I. *What passed between*
Lottie O'Cadhain
and Charles Davies in
their beginning

"WHEN MY MOTHER WAS A YOUNG GIRL SHE spent the pinks of summer evenings sitting on the banks of the Brownies Creek, where it flows into the Cumberland River. She always sat with a ball of worsted in her lap, knitting and dreaming of love coming to her.

The man in her one dream would ride up and surprise her on his horse, and then he would reach down and take the ball of worsted from her and toss it up into the air and shoot a hole through it. Then he would reach out over the horse's head and catch the yarn and hand it back to my mother, saying her beauty pierced such a great place in

3

his heart. Then he would ride off. He never swooped her up and galloped off to a fine house in the Shenandoah Valley and he never hopped down off the horse sheerly to kiss her. He always left. She never let herself dream the story any other way. Even in her dreams my mother denied herself the impossible.

The man who finally wooed my mother wasn't a dream man, and he didn't find her knitting on a river bank. He found her at a Quaker wedding in 1917, which was a very bold place for her to be. Her mother, Bridget O'Cadhain, had taught her daughters that the doors of English churches were the gates of Hell and that terrible things happened to Catholics who went inside, like blindness and deafness or sheerly death. My mother went to the wedding anyway because she was fifteen and therefore a slave to risk.

So there my mother was at the little church, wishing her friends well and being noticed by a young man. He probably spotted her hair right away, which she had knotted and laced with lavender on the cart road, out of her mother's gaze. He introduced himself as Charles Davies and impressed her to the point that by that evening they had decided to court a bit on the sly.

KAYE GIBBONS

A Cure for Dreams

Kaye Gibbons was born in Nash County, North Carolina, and attended North Carolina State University and the University of North Carolina at Chapel Hill. Her first novel, *Ellen Foster*, was awarded the Sue Kaufman Prize of the American Academy and Institute of Arts and Letters and a special citation from the Ernest Hemingway Foundation. Gibbons was awarded the PEN/ Revson Fellowship for *A Cure for Dreams*, and has been the recipient of a National Endowment for the Arts Fellowship. She is also the author of the novel *A Virtuous Woman*. A writer-in-residence at the Library of North Carolina State University, she lives with her three daughters, Mary, Leslie, and Louise, in Raleigh.

KAYE GIBBONS

A Cure for Dreams

A NOVEL

Vintage Contemporaries
Vintage Books
A Division of Random House, Inc.
New York

FIRST VINTAGE CONTEMPORARIES EDITION, JULY 1992

Copyright © 1991 by Kaye Gibbons

Midwife songs taken from *Folks Do Get Born*, by Marie Campbell
(New York: Rinehart, 1946).

Library of Congress Cataloging-in-Publication Data
Gibbons, Kaye, 1960-
    A cure for dreams: a novel / Kaye Gibbons. — 1st Vintage
contemporaries ed.
      p.   cm. — (Vintage contemporaries)
    ISBN 0-679-73672-7 (pbk.)
    I. Title.
[PS3557.I13917C87   1992]
813'.54—dc20   91-50698
               CIP

Manufactured in the United States of America
B9876543

For Louis D. Rubin, Jr.

Acknowledgments

The author wishes to express gratitude to the following organizations and persons: The National Endowment for the Arts; The PEN American Center; The PEN/Revson Foundation; the Federal Writers Project papers in the Southern Historical Collection of the University of North Carolina at Chapel Hill; Susan Nutter and the North Carolina State University Friends of the Library; the November 1989 participants at The North Carolina Center for the Advancement of Teaching; Dudley Jahnke; Jeff Warner, for his permission to quote from "W. P. and A.," contained in *Traditional American Folksongs from the Anne and Frank Warner Collection*, Syracuse University Press, 1984; and Michael, Mary, Leslie, and Louise Gibbons.

A Cure for Dreams

With all our talk of democracy it seems not inappropriate to let the people speak for themselves.

W. T. COUCH
Regional Director
Federal Writers Project
1939

December 15, 1989

Simply enough, my name is Marjorie Polly Randolph. My mother's name was Betty Davies Randolph. At this time I'm forty-seven and a great deal of the time mistaken for much less. This trait I carry from my mother, who carried the trait from her mother, Lottie O'Cadhain Davies. This has always been our fame. My mother died suddenly last month at age sixty-nine, looking no more than sixty.

To tell the truth, she died in a chair talking, chattering like a string-pull doll. I had spent my life listening to her, sometimes all day, which often was my pleasure during snow and long rains. I would need only say to her, Tell me about your mother and you, and Kentucky and Virginia and the wild way I was born. Tell me about the years that made you.

Then she would talk. Talking was my mother's life.

M. P. R.

The Davies were more or less hard-boiled Welsh Quakers who had come to America in the early 1800s. They stayed up in the North and tried to farm, but when they saw they weren't making anything of themselves they started trickling west and south, branch by branch, which has forever been the human tendency. During the Reconstruction after the Slave War, my father's particular branch drifted into Bell County, Kentucky, where everybody in the world was trailing in and yanking up a square of earth, and then my father was born in 1896.

My mother's family, however, had headed to Kentucky the minute they landed in from Galway, and they more or less looked at the valley and the mountains as theirs. They only held papers for a few acres, but still everything within sight seemed to belong to them. And then came flock after flock of Quakers and Methodists and Baptists and even a Lutheran bunch or two.

My mother's people quickly scratched and dug out a little hole and crawled in it and whispered day and night about how everybody in the world, with the exception of the O'Cadhain family and the pope, had never wanted them to have anything. They believed the new people

5

coming pulling cartloads of children and furniture into their little edge of Bell County were merely the last in a long line of snatchers and grabbers. They were very tender about this.

My mother told me a million times that Ireland and the Irish people were special, and that the O'Cadhain family in particular was the most blessed of all because it had been imposed upon without cease since the dawn it sprung up in Galway. For centuries they had been in training to have nothing, so everything was more or less working perfectly according to God's plan.

My mother was not one to glorify in tribulation, and one day she asked herself a question.

If Ireland is a jewel and our family is favored, why are we in Bell County, Kentucky, watching scrawny crops wash down the sides of hills?

She decided to trust the question to her young man, Quaker though he was, who stood and waited for her in the dry creekbed every Sunday afternoon, always holding a spray of lavender. She asked about Ireland and favor and wasted crops, and he told her that Ireland had always overjudged its merits and that her father's scrawny crops washed down hills because he refused to terrace slopes.

Charles told me that if my father would stop sitting around drunk, waiting for God to reverse his notion of water flowing downhill, that our family could be worth at least a little something. He said anything could be had with work, which is what he happened to be morally and physically outfitted for. In school he had gone up as high as the multiplication tables and then dropped himself out of his studies to work. He said that as soon as he learned to walk he became familiar with the hoe and had been in love with work ever since. He said, though, that he also loved me. Everything he said sounded reasonable and true.

Bridget O'Cadhain was no fool. She knew that my mother had taken a sport and he was far from Catholic, but she preferred to let the idea fester while she kept a tighter than usual eye on my mother. Then early one morning Bridget came in from the yard with a fire of wood in her arms and began shoving the pieces of wood in the stove. She saved out the last piece though and turned about and trotted over to the breakfast table and had my mother splay out both hands palms down. She smacked her hands good with the stovewood and then trotted back over and pushed it into the fire. When my mother met her sport

7

that afternoon she told him she'd spent all the previous day learning to use a hammer.

There was so much alcoholic misery in Bridget's life that you would think she'd have been thrilled to work in a Quaker here or Lutheran there to more or less water down this trait. My grandfather, Sheamus, drank fairly all day every day. He was something to behold. My mother woke up every morning to the sound of him yelling for one of his daughters to cook him an egg. He'd stand in the kitchen and shout at the ceiling, Come cook me a goddamn egg! One of the girls would rush in the kitchen and fry the egg. Then my mother's Uncle Bart would roll in and sit at the table. He was very famous in Bell County for sailing as a stowaway from Ireland and swearing incessantly on the Virgin that he consumed only hardtack and forty-two cups of coffee on his way across the ocean. My mother said also that this uncle had purely by accident crawled in the fireplace as a baby, and thus nobody enjoyed looking at him.

My grandfather would shout, Cook Bart a goddamn egg too! Both men would eat their eggs and take to smacking liquor and talking loud-mouthed. The daughters had a very difficult time keeping these men wetted down.

And then Bridget would come in from the wood pile or poultry yard and see them and scream, Jesus, Mary, Joseph! Blessed Virgin, Mother of God! She would drive her husband and brother-in-law away from the table with her yardstick and then swing around and swat and sting the legs of whoever had cooked the eggs.

My mother told me once that her mother was the kind of woman who thought nothing of whipping other people's children. This has always impressed me as something a woman may long to do yet never do. Bridget, though, crossed this line fairly regularly. My mother also told me that her mother was more or less a display of curiosities. I asked her what she meant and then wished I hadn't.

She had very tiny little teeth, like little rodent teeth of some nature, and they were all squared off the same size, like they had been sawed off Zzzzt! all the way across. She trotted from spot to spot. She rarely simply walked. And she always wore black, folds and folds of black, summer and winter.

She refused to learn more than a spattering of English, and when we all sat at the table teaching each other grammar, we would invite our mother to sit down with us, but she would say she didn't need to learn. She didn't want to. Whatever English she picked up from daily living was very

9

flat and twangy in a mountainy way. The only English thing she ever said that sounded like it was said in her true voice was Jesus, Joseph, Mary, Blessed Virgin, Mother of God. She would mix all this in with her Gaelic and chop the kitchen table with her yardstick when we couldn't understand. She had brought her family all the way from Galway to hop in the melting pot and then she refused to melt. This is how stubborn my mother was, and this is also more than likely what gave her the oompth to load everybody up and haul them across the ocean in lieu of starvation in Galway.

I can understand why my mother was perched on ready, hoping for a marriage proposal, which came in 1918. She made her life's commitment to Charles Davies at sixteen and agreed to leave Kentucky with him, bound as she still was to risk.

2. *Lottie's first years of marriage in which she found a baby and cunningly arranged small satisfactions for herself and the child*

"MY FATHER DECIDED HE AND HIS BRIDE WOULD move to North Carolina. I can see him sheerly breathless over the idea of moving himself and a young girl to a new part of the country, working six days a week from can-see to can't-see.

Work and toil may have been my father's bloodtraits but he counted overmuch in the idea that my mother should care as much about making something from nothing as he did. She promised to honor and cherish and obey and all the other, but she never saw the marriage as enrollment for torture. He didn't own her like a plow or a rake. If she wasn't prone to stay at home and let her mother tell her what to do, she certainly wasn't going to take field orders from a young man she had known for a year.

Once I asked my mother, Do you think you ever said or did anything in the creekbed, tarried and dallied or cooed, to the point he would believe he'd found a girl who'd knock herself out working on a farm?

No. Absolutely not.

I said, Then if you didn't promise to work beside him, why did he think you would pull as hard as he pulled?

Because I was a young girl and he knew I loved him, as much as a sixteen-year-old child can love a man. He had told about water flowing forever downhill and he'd told me my father was ignorant and lazy, not cursed. He knew I trusted him and would more than likely yearn for things to do in his favor. He also knew that I knew how to work because Pop drank like he did and left work to the women. He had ridden by our fields and seen me getting up fodder, and he was accustomed to the sight of me and all my sisters, the three who could work plus the three little ones, strewn out across a field like seeds.

Charles rolled all these ideas and sights of me together in his hands and opened them again and saw me there help-

ing him break field boulders with a pickax, saying if we worked like this for the rest of our lives we might die thriving. But instead, when we got to the place in North Carolina I had to tell Charles outright that I had worked in Kentucky and now I wanted a rest. He had very short patience with this. This is certainly not what he had planned. I had thought that marrying him and leaving my school and my sisters would be as plain as spoken words, that I was saying without actually saying, I'm marrying you for love and rest.

I was so young and I already needed to be spelled from labor. Not only did I seek rest, I needed a little baby to help find the rest. In my home, I had always treated my mother's new babies like dolls. I had always taken the least baby to bed with me. Sleep was impossible without a baby in the crook of my arm. Sleep was denied me all night and in the mornings Charles urged me to help him cut down trees and coarse vines all day.

But even if I could've figured out how to get back home, I don't think I would've left. I'd made my choice, and when I was tempted to go back to Bell County, I seemed to hear across the woods and mountains my father screaming for his egg and my mother screaming at me for cooking it. So I decided to stay with Charles and see what would happen to me, and until I understood that I had a hand in making whatever happened happen, I was a very sad young girl.

My father told her that working with him would take her mind off a baby, which was more or less like asking her to sing for her supper. I wouldn't have advised him to do this. During all the time he made her hold out waiting she became very indifferent to him, and in her thinking she began to go her own way. Finally, in 1920 she found her baby, and this was me. By then her affections for my father were all but spoiled.

She did, though, the following year try for another child, but then lost the little fellow within three weeks of the birthing. Thus I actually got to be the baby twice when this one born next to me died. My mother could then have no other babies due to feminine obstacles, but I was not a lonesome child. She was a grand companion. She loved to tell me about myself. I was apparently as good as pie and rarely cried.

And you had one twig of auburn hair. I sewed you a beautiful white cotton petticoat of many layers and a long white gown of piqué. You were never sick a day as a tiny baby although I told your father that your ears were too ten-

der for the wind and thus you couldn't be taken out to the fields. When he believed your ears had had time to harden off, he said, What about now? And I said, No, not now. I told him you had difficulty breathing outdoors. As far as your father knew, you went from ear to eye to nose and throat troubles, and taking you out to a cotton field strapped to my chest would have been your kiss of death. He didn't like you very much from the start, and this is my fault all around. But you weren't liking him very much either. You cried whenever he picked you up. He had big hard hands.

I probably cried because I was accustomed to being held in a happy fashion, and the way I bunched up around my father didn't stop when I was out of his arms and then crawling and then walking. He put me off continuously. I remember one afternoon sitting on a rug, drawing pictures from out of a book and enjoying my mother chitter-chattering when he came in from work. When the door closed behind him, I thought, He's come home to ruin our day. I assumed this was his intention. This was my first original thought of my father.

He was only happy once a year, after a crop was in and sold and after he'd squeezed every bit of gristmill money he could from his customers. By the time I was six or seven, I linked September and dry maple leaves blowing across our yard with my father's only time of pleasure.

He'd sit at the supper table and say, Yes, this time-a-year all I'm thinking about is who all do I owe money to and who all and how much is owing me.

Then he'd take out his pocketbook and give my mother and me money and tell us that would be all the money we'd see for another year. But we knew better. My mother always managed to come up with more than her allowance, and she always managed to explain her doings nicely.

My mother loved fabric, and since my father would never have known the price difference between organdy or chintz or chiffon, she educated him as she saw fit. In September when he was so enthusiastic about life and the world and even his wife and child, my mother would take the money he gave us to town and buy something like a beautiful length of chintz and come home and school him.

Charles, the gingham was through the roof. Through the roof! So I did you a favor and bought this. I know it seems incredible that a simple cotton runs more than chintz. I could hardly believe it myself. But the looming mills, from what I understand, have had a hard time getting rid of chintz, it being so bold, and they've had to mark the bolts down to almost nothing. I'm not thrilled with it, but the gingham was high as a cat's back, and Betty's simply splitting out of her old clothes like a grasshopper. She had to have something to wear! I don't mind going about gaudy to save you money, and neither does she. We're both glad to do it.

He'd mumble and grumble about how his mother would never have worn anything so ugly, and then he'd go back out and work, work, work the rest of the year, waking at four and calling it morning, leaving home and coming home daily in the dark. When September came back around my mother and I would go out again and handle every bolt of fabric in town and come home with Venice lace passing for irregular eyelet and beaded English netting passing for outdated and unwanted millinery stock.

The two salesladies we dealt with understood that this was our folly, and often we would get home and see that buttons and ribbon had been hidden in the bottoms of our boxes. We occasionally sat with these two women behind the counter and ate candy, unpaid for, and scrutinized pattern books. This is where, I'm sure, I learned to recognize style, and I still tend to link style with Butterick's and McCall's pattern books and lovely piece candies pressed into shapes.

I know that for myself I felt very guilty at times about the deceit, but when my mother and I were pinning and basting a lovely chintz up on each other and I saw how happy she was, I felt nothing but pleasure. There was no pleasure in life for my father, but that wasn't our fault. We didn't plant in him a thirst for work. He said God and his family inspired him to strive, in spite of the fact that he didn't keep up with his relations and he never went to church. His gristmill served as church, and he'd go there on Sunday and sweep and repair, wishing it was Monday.

I more or less slipped into his work-and-earn-all-you-can frame of mind when I was about nine or ten, though just for a moment. From the back of Grier's Almanac I secretly applied for a case of rosebud salve, which avowed to do marvelous things for the complexion but merely smelled good. I grew lazy and uninterested, as children will, and let it set and set and didn't sell it. It sat unopened on the pantry shelves with all the beets and pickles and stewed tomatoes, and then my father decided he'd like a jar of something and, very out of character, got it himself. And, of course, there was the box. My mother hopped in on my behalf and promised I would sell the salve immediately, and in one afternoon she got rid of the entire case. She sold a few jars at the store, though most of the salve she sold to herself, and thus my mother smelled of roses well into the Depression.

3. *Of the child's refusal*
to maintain a steady diet,
including further notice
of the mother's unyielding
disposition towards
the father

"I N TALKING TO ME, MY FATHER CALLED THE SUM-
mer of 1932, The time your mother let you get sick.
Like many young girls at twelve, I seemed to lose my ap-
petite due to changes in my nature, and instead of encour-
aging my system to enjoy different healthful foods, I kept
to a very limited menu. I didn't know any better.

I developed a taste for corn bread and molasses, and
soon these were the only foods that would please me. My
mother tried to prime me with tidbits of other vegetables
or meats, but I declared I would eat what I wanted or
nothing at all. So while I ate truly heaps of corn bread and

gobs of molasses, she and my father would fight. He'd tell her that hogs and cows ate a more varied diet than me.

My mother would yell, *The child's got to fill up on something! I'm surprised you're not grateful for her eating so cheaply!*

Like other mothers of this time, she wasn't born knowing about vitamins or taught nutrition at school, so she honestly believed that as long as I was full I was fine. The way you're trained is the way you're trained, and so ill-eating habits passed with ease through generations. Not long before this time a man had come around running for Congress, promising everyone he'd replace fatback with steaks and loins, and he lost our precinct. People couldn't throw their votes behind a candidate who threatened to take away their food. Most everyone was of this mind.

As this went on and on through the summer I began looking and feeling very indifferent compared to the way I usually did. My skin was red and crisp in spots, and all I wanted to do was sleep. All the time. All I cared to do was sleep stretched out in a misery faint on my bed.

My mother located the doctor who merely hit the high spots checking me. He said my skin was no more than sunburned and my tiredness and weight loss were more or less popular female complaints, for which tonics abounded. He told my mother to make me wear long sleeves and a hat in the sun and eat more gravy. The topic of my menu never arose.

So the next day my mother covered me up for the sun and dosed me up with Lydia Pinkham until I fairly reeled from the alcohol. She kept asking my father if he thought I looked like I was getting better, and he'd say, I've already told you what's wrong with her.

By this time, if she had developed the urge to agree with him, she fought it. So thus cutting her nose off, she continued to let me eat as I pleased, and I stayed wrapped in the sun and sheerly intoxicated by my medication. But my skin failed to improve and my tongue, of all things, started to interfere with my talking. Upon examination in my father's shaving mirror, I noticed my tongue was swollen and somewhat dark, which was quite frightening for me.

My mother got the doctor back out to our house and told him in no uncertain terms to do what he was paid to do. One sight inside my mouth and he announced that I was suffering from pellagra. He said it had lately reared its head among the lower classes, and he was frankly surprised that people like ourselves who could afford a good home, nice clothes, and an automobile could let themselves get in this fix. He said that when he examined me before that my case hadn't progressed enough to judge accurately, and then he reported horror stories of children in the later stages of advancement, all told with an eye to my mother. He put me on liver extract tablets right away and gave my mother a great deal of advice on how to feed a child, all told as well in a belittling fashion. Then he said he was going to stop at the mill and discuss this matter with my father. I recall longing at that moment to be swept up by a cyclone.

I expected my mother to tell the doctor that if he'd noticed the illness when he came out the first time and gave me the once-over-lightly that I wouldn't be in this fix, but she didn't. She listened and nodded, a scarce behavior, and even more scarce, she apologized for telling him earlier to do what he was paid to do. She even paid for the second visit in spite of what I know she believed was a bungled first look. I wondered if she was sincere or if she was more or less fawning to convince him not to visit my father at his job. Though I could usually read my mother, on this call she eluded me.

But the doctor went straightaway to the mill, and my father came home early with a rude air, obviously glorifying in the memory of my mother yelling, *The child's got to fill up on something!* He walked right by me lying on the sofa and stood in front of my mother and wouldn't leave her alone until he'd teased her into saying she didn't know anything about anything, nothing at all.

I know, I thought I knew about children, but I don't know anything, nothing, not a thing, not a thing about nothing. Then she flew into the pine thicket and stayed there a while to try to get the shame off of her.

I got better quickly on the liver extract. And, needless to say, my mother sat and watched me eat all the niacin foods the doctor had written out for us. Her mood improved with my health although she seemed to step backwards each time she heard that summer referred to as the time she let me get sick. Once I actually saw her put a hand out for balance when my father said this.

For my birthday that October she gave me a little book of poems. I'm sure none of them are worth much, though some were very dramatic when read with the correct tone, which my mother had, particularly when she read her favorite one, "The Tide Rises, The Tide Falls," with the sea and the darkness and the darkness and the sea, which I didn't go for.

The best poem though was on the inside of the front cover, which she had inscribed to me. She had gone to great lengths to write it beautifully. In fact, I had to ask her to read it aloud to me. I couldn't make out the words for all the letters looped and whirled back on themselves. So she read:

> *If ever a husband you should have*
> *And this book he should see*
> *Tell him of all our youthful days*
> *And kiss him once for me.*

My mother indeed had a very artful hand, and anyone who couldn't read or write depended on her to do their writing and fill out their medical papers and aid forms as they arose. I read over a great deal of what she wrote and tried to explain the value of at least a little punctuation, though this went by her. She'd wave me aside and say it didn't matter.

After she had filled out a form she would have the person make their mark, and then she would get herself fixed squarely in front of the table and co-sign her own name with great swirls and flourishes, like every Dependent Children form was a peace treaty. Then she would blow on the paper until she was satisfied that the ink was dry and then she would inspire whoever was watching to comment on her signature. She would tell them how she was always at the front of her class though she neglected to tell them that she had stopped attending her old field school at fifteen and had since more or less renounced the apostrophe and comma. I witnessed this one thousand times.

4. *Feminine secrets disclosed*

"MY MOTHER EASED FURTHER AWAY FROM MY father so thus he had less and less time to talk about my illness or anything else to her. Her intent, in fact, was to leave him without leaving him. Soon we were living more outside our home than in.

In the afternoons after my school let out, she and I would strike out walking and return home barely in time to lay out the meals that Polly Deal had already served my father for lunch and left on the stove disguised as supper. Polly Deal was a wonderful gingercake-colored woman who worked as our part-time cook and laundress and doubled as a midwife and baby doctor.

The most clever trick was for Polly to serve a bland boiled chicken at lunch and then leave the leftovers for my mother to lay forth six hours later muddled in with some canned stuff. For years I watched my mother fairly teeter on the edge of having my father ask her where she'd been all afternoon that she couldn't fix a fresh meal at supper, but he never noticed for his senses were dulled in this regard.

My mother and I seemed to go in one person's house and out of another's, stepping into most houses without knocking, merely calling, Woo Hoo! She knew everything everybody had and where they kept it. She could've put her hands on rolling pins and colanders in the dark. She knew to the date when women would need their knives sharpened.

Her goal was to organize a gang of women for a habitual social hour, though this plan met with difficulty when woman after woman said, We'll have to meet elsewhere, for I'm ashamed of my house. As homes were in the grip of Mr. Hoover and his Depression, these women meant what they said.

My mother solved the problem by selecting Porter's store

for the meetings, the back of which served as kitchen and sitting room for Porter and his wife, Celia. So thus five or so women more or less chartered the meetings, and though things got off to a rousing start, after three gatherings they exhausted things to discuss and spent most of the hour offending Mr. Hoover, which wore thin on Celia, the one Republican present and the owner of the table and chairs and the coffee pot.

My mother thought and thought, and finally thought of everyone's playing cards, which was looked upon by some as immoral, if not for the gambling then for the pleasure women received from something other than home and hearth. All were shocked when my mother insisted on betting, though they became jolly after she convinced them that families couldn't starve over the likes of pennies. So they reached into their apron pockets and pulled out their little dabs of egg and pin money, twirled and tied in the corners of cotton handkerchiefs, and listened to my mother explain odds. Her father and uncle, as was to be expected, were big on cards and my mother had soaked up everything they said. I fast became an excellent player. My mother bragged to some that I could hold my own aboard a riverboat.

My father hated gambling or anything at all involving the luck of the draw. My mother's method with him was to swear to stop and then pretend for weeks that she had merely watched the games without playing, and then he would bring home a rumor that she'd played, dealt, and even taught those interested pinochle. Then she'd say she was weak at heart and agree to stay at home the next Saturday afternoon, but the next week he'd slacken his watch and off she'd go to play cards until she was caught again. This process rotated around perhaps six or seven times, and impressed me at thirteen years old as a very trying way to organize one's relationship.

Sometimes when my mother and I walked about the community in the late afternoon we would stop in the road in front of houses, and she'd tell me if the women inside were happy or sad, if they were loved or not loved by men. She would tell me secrets she suspected and sometimes she would slip me suspicions that women had revealed as the truth. This was very, very educating. She would look at a house and say, for instance, *Martha's passing as loved, which must be tiring.* My mother, of course, had given up trying to pass. Everyone knew or knew of my father and how he lived to squeeze pennies out of people, and everyone knew that he loved work and gain more than his family.

Other women's news wasn't always bad, however. One time my mother told me that a particular friend, Amanda Bethune, was loved more than a usual amount by her husband and that this husband would lie down and die for Amanda if called to.

Can you believe it, Betty? They've been married for ten years and no trace of love has rubbed off, not a trace. I wouldn't know what to do with a man like that. I wouldn't know what to do with a man who did more than show up for meals. I wonder where she found him.

I thought my mother's idea of Amanda's love was built on the memories of all the times her husband Richard had come in the store and given her a piece of money for extras and looked the other way concerning her cards, all the times I'd heard her remark of this thing and that she'd been given. Up until our community met Mr. Boll Weevil, Amanda left her children with her mother once a year and headed down to Warm Springs with her sister for hot water soakings, her annual birthday gift from Richard. Also, at Easter he habitually sent Amanda's hats to Charleston for trimmings that surpassed her dreams, and each spring she wore these hats and posed with her children for the man who came around Kodaking. All-in-all, nothing seemed too good for Amanda, and in spite of all she received she was kind.

My mother said, though, that these gifts weren't true signs of Richard's feelings. *Money doled out in public this way could possibly hide the worst kinds of secrets galore.*

I said, Then what is the sign? How can you look at your friends and tell if they're loved right?

Listen and hear what the men call their wives when they come to the store to fetch them. Listen. Old squaw. This sounds bad but it's truly sweet. Dear and Honey. I wouldn't trust these. They have an unnatural ring. No name. Just, Come on! This is what your father says, so that should tell you something. And this is what Roy Duplin says calling for Sade, and you know how nasty this sounds. Watch Sade's shoulders hop the next time he yells for her. At least your father's call has no kind of tone attached to it, which is almost worse. Rarely, rarely though will you hear a woman called from the store by her name, which is best. So listen for each time Richard Bethune comes to the door and calls, Amanda! so nicely. And watch how she gladly goes to him. A woman's name will always suffice, but if you'll keep your ears open in a room with men and women, you'll hear it's the call used least often.

5. *An account of things which
heretofore were unsaid, or
a lesson for the tardy*

"A S LESS AND LESS MONEY CAME INTO OUR COM-
munity, the more it seemed that men felt the desire
to be perfectly wild with women. Every week it seemed
that we heard a new tale of a man putting his foot wrong.
I even still tend to associate unfaithfulness with despera-
tion, each urge attached to the other like moss on bark.

The Crash daily drilled the idea into some people's heads
that they were destined never to have anything. Automobiles, food, housing, and children's shoes cost more money
than many men on Milk Farm Road simply had, but
Willifordtown mill tarts presented themselves for so little

that they may as well have been free. All a community needed was one tart to make men feel like they'd survived the Crash with a measure of looks and attraction, which wasn't the same as cash solvency but gave the same sort of thrill as unbridled spending.

Sade Duplin, who had never hurt anybody, had to contend with a tart. She was already on the verge of losing the farm her father had passed to her, and then she was handed the task of putting her roving husband back in order. One morning she became overwrought in our home and thus ignored my youthful presence in telling her very chilling affairs to my mother.

She said, Since nature left me Roy has lost interest.

Sade had taken a hysterectomy early and had thus been thrown into the change, and Roy apparently viewed her as suddenly old. My mother said this was ridiculous, and then she asked Sade what she planned to do about this girl, as if Sade had commented on fleas or ants or spider mites, and my mother was curious as to Sade's preference of straight boric acid or mint jellied arsenic. *Have you ever had this problem before? What do you think will work best on it?*

Sade told her that there wasn't anything she could do,

that she didn't have what it took to throw Roy back in line. By the time Roy dragged home off a date past midnight, Sade's hard day had long sucked and drained her of the energy it would take to deal with him. My mother, however, abounded in energy, and though she said nothing to Sade, I could see that she intended to do something large to rectify the situation.

The only thing cheaper than a next-to-free tart was talk, so my mother decided Sade's interests could best be served by passing about a very nasty story of this Willifordtown girl's negative Wassermann reaction. And in two nights Roy was home before dark, no doubt tortured over the prospects of his own health, probably scouring the insides of his cheeks for white patches and making up reasons why Sade shouldn't sleep next to him, which she must have lost her taste for doing the minute he put his foot wrong.

Soon he eased back into his work. My mother didn't mention the problem specifically again to Sade and certainly not her solution. She merely let nature take its course. And when she one day asked Sade very casually how things were at home, she answered, Fine. Although Roy still stood at the front of the store and boomed, Come on! and yanked

Sade away from rummy, we all simply took this as a sign that their lives were moving back to normal.

But then the next year Roy was murdered, and while dead is dead and crisis enough, murder always seems worse. My mother had commented to me several times that Roy was more or less a lightning rod for tragedy. Besides taking company with another woman and treating his wife so nastily in public, he also had a reputation for whipping his work animals without mercy, and we had always heard that a man who imposes on animals will soon be imposed upon himself. As well, he robbed his tenants blind and had absolutely no race manners. All in all, he was more or less an unsavory person.

Everything happened on a Friday evening. My mother and I were at a hundred-year-old lady's birthday dinner, when John Carroll, who served as a part-time deputy sheriff, came in the house and asked to borrow my mother from the party. I remember him being very serious in fending off everyone's cake offers. He talked in my mother's ear, and I can still see all those women, including myself and the hundred-year-old lady, staring, trying to make out his lips.

Everybody went to the coat closet with my mother and

took a hand in slipping on her jacket. She whispered to us that the trouble was at Sade Duplin's house. *Sade sent word for John to bring me when he goes to the house. It appears that Roy has just been shot and killed.* We all thought, Oooo! though we tried to hide it.

My mother made me wait, oh, years, for all the details of exactly how Roy was imposed upon. And then after she finally told me everything, she made me swear not to tell, which was like asking me to carry a bomb in my mouth. As much as we both enjoyed talk, this is one thing that simply couldn't be told with Sade alive and perfectly a sitting duck for justice, but now I can be free to tell.

My mother said that she and John Carroll got to the Duplin house about eight-thirty and found Roy Duplin simply shot to pieces in the yard. Sade was drooped all over the kitchen table, crying, with both hands in front of her on the table, turning them over and under, over and under, watching them through her crying as if she expected a surprise to appear the next turn. She appeared very glad to see my mother and soon calmed her flipping hands. John left the two women inside and then he went about outside looking for his clues. But while he was in the yard crouched over with a lantern, searching for bullet casings and footprints and all the other kinds of things a man would naturally look for, my mother was inside fixing Sade chamomile tea and getting ideas.

She noticed right away that Sade's plate was dirty and Roy's plate was clean. The solitary pot on the stove was covered, but she smelled a nice beef stew. There was a pie on the counter and only one piece had been cut out, not a man's serving but the size of piece a woman will have when she just wants a little sliver. And it had been removed neatly, which made it a woman's slice all the more.

Then my mother left Sade at the table sipping on her tea and strolled about the house. She looked into the back bedroom and noticed a half-finished quilt on the loom and naturally had to examine it. Sade had been describing her new Dutch doll variation for weeks and everyone's curiosity was up. So my mother naturally started looking at it and admiring it, and then she saw that the last twenty or thirty stitches were very wild and uneven and made no sense at all. She thought, *A woman would have to be extremely disturbed to sew that raggedly, and she would have to be sheerly distracted out of her mind to leave this slipshod stitching in.* Then she sat down on a stool and pulled out the ugly stitches and fixed them right, listening all the time to Sade wailing in the kitchen.

My mother had been to her share of funerals and knew the varying pitches of wives' wails, the sounds made for husbands corrupted with cancer, knocked down by strokes and heart attacks, bitten by water moccasins, or gored by crazy bulls. In our community, these were the ways men had died. There wasn't a great deal of variety in the way people lived or died, either one. When she heard Sade's very peculiar cry, she said to herself, *This is neither the cry of a woman startled by death or relieved that it has finally come.*

Then she imagined how she would sound if she'd just murdered my father, which may or may not have taken a great deal of imagination, and this is what she heard coming from the kitchen. She heard a woman being afraid, in the main, of being caught. Then she knew exactly what had happened. She said she could see everything that had taken place.

Sade had waited for Roy to come in on time for supper and finally she gave up and ate alone. She waited some more and then went ahead and had dessert. By the time a woman eats pie alone she has long been pushed past her point. Sade cooked lavish pies. Pies and cakes take a great deal of trouble and historically have never been viewed as something merely to eat. Forced to eat by herself, this was exactly the nonchalant way Sade was being asked to view her craft.

So there she sat alone, thinking about the insult of Roy not coming to the house for supper, in light of the fact that for years he had rudely jerked her away from her friends in the prime of her Saturday afternoons. And she probably thought about him with his Willifordtown girl and wondered if she was why he was late, as she had been many, many times before. And she had to, I'm sure, think about how Roy had run her two oldest children away from home. She probably sat and picked at her nice pie and went over every other humiliation and embarrassment, both public and private, though most likely dwelling on the public times.

And then when Roy still didn't come in, she got up and went to work on her quilt while she still had a little bit of light. The room with the quilt had a nice west window. Sitting there at her loom, Sade got madder and madder about the supper and the day and her general life with Roy and without her children. And seeing him walk down the path towards the house, her stitches veered and jerked about on her pattern chalk line. Roy probably saw her too, and he probably yelled something at her in his throaty raspy voice.

Then the thought more than likely dawned on Sade of how easy it would be to kill him and be rid of him. And then she took the shotgun out from under the bed and propped the gun on the windowsill and shot Roy a few times, probably in the midst of his yapping at her. Then she collected the casings and moved them where she saw fit, cleaned and reloaded the gun and put it back under the bed, and waited for it to cool down before she sent for help.

When John Carroll asked her what she knew about Roy's death, she reported that she had stepped down through the wheat field to the pond to sit after supper, and then when she got back to the house she found Roy. My mother said she glanced down at Sade's cotton stockings but saw no picks nor burrs nor dandelion seedwings. Sade also reported about a rover her husband had run off from prowling about that morning, and in describing the man she was careful to describe a thousand men on the tramp. Men on the tramp weren't uncommon, and sharing everyone's view of rovers, John Carroll remarked, The fellow must have gotten a gun and come back mad.

He didn't know to examine cotton stockings for briar picks, and he didn't know how to see and judge clean and dirty plates, slivers of cut pie, wild stitches, and wailing. This had more to do with the fact that he was full-time male than it did with the fact that he was merely part-time deputy and neither bright nor curious. Details escaped him.

He put together a shoddy search for the rover, which was stopped soon after it started when my father and other men said getting their crops in the house was more urgent than looking for an unknown who was surely already up as far as Baltimore. And their unspoken attitude was also: And besides, Roy was such a sonofabitch.

After Roy was buried, several of us went and helped Sade dole out his clothes to some colored men, and what they didn't want she pressed them to take anyway. She cleaned out his belongings very quickly. Then we all had pie, and at the time I didn't think about it, but now I know why my mother was making overmuch of the crust.

Neighborhood women took turns staying with Sade for

weeks and weeks after Roy died. She was afraid to stay in the house alone, which with hindsight isn't surprising. We had all heard, Mean in life, meaner in death. Some nights Sade's companions had to dose her up with double and triple doses of paregoric to get her to sleep. Fear of seeing Roy Duplin or John Carroll either one at her window was more than enough to make Sade lose her reason, but she didn't.

After a while she regained her bearings. She got clearer and clearer-eyed and more and more calm, and if I had only met her for the first time I wouldn't have believed a word of her secret. In fact, I'm sure people actually meeting her anew put her in the category of women who chose a single life, who live in the same house with a cat or a bird or the like all their lives and seem to be so content with everything so still. And later, once word spread that Roy was gone, Sade's oldest children came back and visited and kept coming back visiting, bringing boxes of stockings and sea foam taffy and a damask bed jacket and all sorts of other wonderful things.

As months passed, Sade used all the money she discovered hoarded and made Roy's room over into a pretty little parlor. Living, he'd never let her have a smidgen of fluff.

She put the quilt on a daybed in this room, and although my mother was in this room and touched this quilt maybe five hundred times, she and Sade never said a word to each other about the fixed reckless stitching.

6. *A brief account which treats matters relating to courtship on Milk Farm Road*

"AFTER SADE'S PROBLEM WAS SOLVED AND HER house was more or less in order, my mother could've ridden out the rest of the Depression keeping to herself. However, she believed it was important that she continue to stay alert and keep up with the community, as with Sade, and also keep up with herself.

My mother was determined that neither one of us would go downhill and lose all thought of appearance. She continued to roll my hair as well as her own every night and she still waxed her legs as necessary, a habit she'd secretly acquired from a ladies' book. Her other alternative was to sit around the kitchen table all morning with holes in her stockings, drinking watered-down coffee, which was the state we found more and more women in, even Amanda Bethune, who in 1928 had been declared as having it all. Of course, my mother took one look at Amanda, yanked her up, brought her back to our house, and lent her a chintz skirt and her faux ruby barrette.

Although particular people in the community talked about my mother as being silly and viewed her high spirit in the same vein as telling jokes at a funeral, she was merely refusing to let herself wallow in the times. And this particular bunch who looked at my mother sidewise in her high colors were the same ones who lived to load up in an automobile and spend Saturdays at the pictures. My mother, however, was a walking, talking, free moving picture, and people looked and listened to see what she would wear and what she would say the same way they sat in the Centre Theatre and stared at the screen, waiting for the story to start.

I was in step with my mother, and though I was on friendly terms with young people my age, I preferred to stay right by her like a little twin. My teachers considered me smart and pretty and said as much on my reports, although they often noted that I wasn't an outgoing mixer or mingler and joined few clubs. I had hit the first grade running and moved right on through like I was born to go to school. But still, I was well liked enough to suit me. I merely preferred my mother's company to people in my age category, which some confused with haughtiness or lack of school spirit.

And in my teenaged years I didn't develop the drive that drives some girls from sport to sport. Some boys spread the impression that I thought I was better than them, which wasn't true in the main. I flirted with a few in school, though I never dreamed of marrying or even kissing any of them. I didn't care for them, good-natured though they were. It was very hard for me to ride next to one of these boys on a Sunday afternoon pony cart outing after seeing him on Saturday afternoon, sweating and stripped to the waist, yanking along behind a one-horse plow. Other girls didn't seem to have a problem with it, and so they all packed in for joyrides or went to the State Fair and yanked around laughing in the tilt-a-whirl. Instead, I sat beside my mother in women's houses and laughed along with Lum and Abner while they all wondered what I saw in Bing. Affairs with young men overall, as a rule, held not a great deal of interest for me.

The only one of the pack I would've ever come close to loving was Luther Miracle, and I think I was first interested in him solely because of the name. If I'd married him I'd be named Betty Miracle. Luther wasn't much to look at but he was one of a courteous few, polite as a basket of chips. When I was sixteen I told my mother about feelings I was starting to have about Luther, and she didn't like it a bit. She poured out her distaste for Luther.

His hair's always dirty. Locks and locks of filthy hair. It's a sign of lax character. Have you ever seen him clean? And listen to this! His mother elbowed her way into a card game last Saturday and tried to cheat, which actually surprised nobody. I was told she stopped going to her Sunday School after she was caught putting an improper donation in the birthday box. His father lets Charles cheat him and won't do anything to stop it. I'd do without before I'd go with Luther Miracle, though I do like the ring of Betty Miracle. But there's always still his hair.

She had all grades of evidence against Luther Miracle. When we were at cards the next week, without Mrs. Miracle's attendance, my mother asked the other women to back her up on the Miracle family, and they did. If I had taken Luther Miracle as my sport, I would've known exactly what I was in for, all my future circumstances checked off on a fairly accurate list put together by the rummy women.

Even if our mothers didn't tell us everything outright, we had learned to read some signs about young men for ourselves. We knew what would be in store if we courted or married a boy whose father liked to drink more than a little. Or if a boy came to school every day with a beautiful lunch in his bucket, the girls knew he'd be looking to marry his mother, and girls with that kind of instinct would run to pair off with him, and they'd court with everybody's blessings. If a boy never wanted to take off his shirt at recess, this was because of buggy whip or razor strap scars his father had left and the boy would more than likely be drawn to do the same to his own children and more than likely his wife. He was harder to mate, but nothing was impossible. It was very difficult for a young person to lie about his character on Milk Farm Road. And all this information was traded freely between women with daughters, like meringue secrets or geranium cuttings.

7. *Of Trudy's bold appearance and Lottie and Betty's first sally into the Woodlief home*

"I HAD NO CLOSE FRIENDS AT ALL, MALE OR FE-male, until 1937 when Trudy Woodlief moved her family to Milk Farm Road. She and I became good friends despite the fact that I was seventeen and she was twenty-eight with several children.

My mother first told me about Trudy, who had blown into the store and more or less announced that she intended to have credit. Though it battered Porter's nerves to deny poor women credit, deny her he did, and thus Trudy left the store in a rage. People we knew didn't fall into fast rages. They simmered, as with Sade, or wormed around trouble, as with my mother. Rarely did I witness a tantrum or open fight of any public nature. Maybe it had something to do with the heat and our desire not to stir up the temperature. But Trudy apparently swung her arms and stomped and what-have-you, thus early on making a wild name for herself. My mother said she was afraid the incident took years off of Porter's life. He was exceptionally gentle.

My mother finished describing Trudy to me and recruited me to walk down the hill with her to stick our head in the door. As usual, we were not to go empty-handed so we put some canned peaches and tomatoes together with a good portion of a wonderful ham. Such lean ham was a great rarity, and of even greater rarity was the fact that my mother had baked it herself.

We walked down the hill and up to the house. We could see through the screen door all the way to the three yardbabies and two older girls in the back, all already dirty, yet rolling about in even more dirt. Trudy was in the front room, wearing a very chewed-up-looking robe, with one leg high up on a bureau, smoking a cigarette and shaving her legs with lotion and a straight razor. I was thrilled, yet scared to go inside and probably would not have had my mother not urged me through the door.

We knocked on the door and Trudy slunk over and invited us in, not at all modest in her robe. She had that washed-out, cheapy sort of look that some men can call pretty. My mother was examining everything as hard as she could, Trudy as well as the house.

Towards the food, Trudy acted as if she was more or less bored with people bringing her baked hams. She told me I could put everything on the kitchen table, which I did, but only after stacking plate upon plate. When I went back into the living room my mother was asking Trudy a thousand questions of every nature. Trudy, however, was hovered over her legs and only answered my mother if it was convenient with her smoking. I was amazed that she could even attempt to do so much at once, keeping the cigarette in her mouth talking, shaving with a straight razor, yelling at her children through the door.

She managed to answer my mother to say she'd come from Baton Rouge. And as soon as she said this my mother shot me a look to say, *Oh my goodness! What will we do with somebody from Louisiana?* Louisiana had always been the place that no matter how miserable your life was you could always say, At least I'm not from Louisiana. We always had the impression that people in Louisiana were practicing tropical voodoo, marrying their sisters, and voting for Huey Long all day. Overall, it seemed like a very frightening place to be from.

My mother asked her if everything she'd heard about Louisiana and voodoo was true. *You know, hair balls driving grown men crazy and things of that nature.*

Trudy thought about it and then told us that right before they left Louisiana her grandfather had died and she had made her oldest daughter lean over in the coffin, pick up the dead man's hand, and press it to a strawberry scar on her neck. She said everybody at the wake went Wooo! when it faded.

We also learned that Trudy and her husband, Tommy, had picked up and hauled northward and gotten wind of work in Gordon Randolph's orchards, and so they came and were given the nicest house they'd ever had. She was thrilled with their windowscreens, and thus far things were going lovely, with the one exception that Porter wouldn't extend her credit.

My mother defended Porter, who had fallen on hard times to the point that the cash register people repossessed his cash register, leaving Porter reduced to making change out of his wife's muffin tin. She explained to Trudy that Porter was in no shape to operate on credit. We expected Trudy to say she understood and she'd have to get by the best she could. But she didn't. She said, Fine! Damn him then! And then she threw her other leg up on the bureau and proceeded to smear lotion on it.

She said, Listen, I've still got this leg to go and then feed people. How about y'all get ready and go on?

Though my mother was shaken by Trudy asking us to leave in such a point-blank manner, she had her mind enough to say, *Fine, but let me collect my pan if you don't mind.*

Trudy organized her cigarettes and razor blade and walked towards the kitchen with my mother and I following behind, my mother whispering in my ear all through the long house. *Maybe that's how they get rid of company in Louisiana. Maybe they just ask people to leave!*

When we reached the kitchen we saw all five children taking turns looking under the lid of our pan, pretending to choke, gagging themselves, and making wild faces at my mother. Trudy slapped a few fingers out of mouths and lifted the lid herself. Then she looked my mother square forward and said, They hate ham. They'd rather eat dirt than a ham. Too bad it's not a hen.

In, oh, seconds my mother and I were halfway up the hill to our house, pulling the ham, the peaches, and tomatoes in the same wagon that had borne it downhill before.

I said, I don't suppose she'll be invited to play cards? I don't suppose they'll be asked to taffy pulls?

No! Phooey!

She yanked the wagon on home barely in time for my father to come home and remark at this odd supper of ham and peaches and cold tomatoes. My mother started to cry. *I've never known a meal to be so persecuted!* Then she excused herself and thus I excused myself and walked out behind her.

8.

A further account of the Woodlief family, including Lottie's first compassion for them all, with the one exception of the husband

"I'VE ALWAYS ENJOYED THE COMPANY OF MORE unusual people than most, simply listening to them and looking at them, so thus I felt drawn without control back to the Woodlief household. My mother, though, told me in no uncertain terms to conquer the urge to go down the hill.

Even though she hadn't talked to Trudy but that one time, she liked her less and less every day. She told Sade and Amanda and all the rest several times exactly how high Trudy had her leg up on the bureau. Everybody, particularly those overweight, was stunned. These were the kind of women who liked to believe that God has very definite ideas about who should be fat and who should be thin. So, when they featured Trudy, so lean, with her leg up to her shoulders, shaving, they felt doomed.

I waited and kept my distance from the Woodliefs, according to my mother's wishes. The Woodliefs kept a great deal to themselves as well. But then after about eight or nine or so months, the children fell into a sheer stealing frenzy, stealing anything they could lift to carry, even down to laundry off the line. Women were very embarrassed over having to go down the hill and ask the children to hand back socks and petticoats. I heard one woman say she would've much rather sent her husband to bring things home, but she was frankly afraid Trudy would drag him bodily into the house and corrupt his affections for her.

Trudy's husband, Tommy, stole in a very brazen manner as well, stealing first dogs and then copper, stripping it and then hoarding it in back of his house in broad daylight. My mother had predicted he would do something like this. We'd passed him several times walking, and she whispered to me that Tommy was of an undesirable element.

He's got criminal blood. He looks like he'd love to go right now and rob a bank.

How do you know?

I can tell.

You can't tell anything. You simply can't give anybody the benefit of the doubt.

Why do I have to? Where is it written that I have to give somebody with criminal blood the benefit of the doubt?

Before John Carroll could think through the copper problem, Tommy loaded it up and sold it and off he went. He just took his foot in his hand and left his wife six months along with twins, with already enough kids to bait a trotline.

This threw my mother into an awkward spot. When news of Tommy Woodlief abandoning his family reached the rummy table, she stopped us in the midst of collecting pennies for a fresh deck to announce her change in attitude. *No matter how filthy this young woman keeps her house and children, no matter how rude she is and how mean her children are, certainly no woman deserves to be fooled up with twins and left stranded.*

Everybody, especially Sade, yelled, Whew! What a bum!

My mother promised them that by the end of the day she'd think of the best way to help. She believed Trudy would be peculiar about community aid, although little did she know that, the second Tommy left, Trudy walked all the way to town to push for Dependent Children checks. My mother developed the same stern face as she had thinking up the Wassermann solution, the same look as when she yanked the crying, newly poor Amanda Bethune up from her table and restored her self-regard, and certainly the same look as when she explained betting to women so they could have a little thrill on a Saturday afternoon. Mr. Roosevelt's programs were very helpful, but I'm sure he never realized how much women like my mother were doing to help him pick up after Mr. Hoover.

Later that afternoon, as though my mother's thinking so hard on Trudy's situation had pulled her to the store, she appeared, smoking and swayback, and she proceeded straight to the counter to hound Porter again about credit. We weren't used to seeing women smoke, pregnant or otherwise.

Trudy said to Porter, I'm asking again for credit.

Porter said more than likely for the sixth time that week that he had pulled in all his accounts and couldn't set up any new ones. He said he couldn't make any exceptions, that he and Celia had to make a living, and he started rambling, overexplaining himself. And then Trudy slammed the flat of her hand on the counter and shouted out loud, Fine! Damn! Then she called the children in from playing in the dust outside. They appeared splinter barefoot and more or less clambered over each other coming through the door. Then they broke apart and shot out and slipped behind various counters like pool balls, extending themselves credit.

Porter was a very fragile man and had difficulty handling anything out of the range of normal, so thus he was robbed of fruity chews and all-day suckers and sheer pocketfulls of ten-for-a-pennies. Celia was braver in this regard and got up from the card table and encouraged the children to unload themselves.

None of this fazed Trudy, who had come back to the living room section of the store and walked around the card table, wishing somebody would make over her and the recent news of her carrying twins. She had previously told us that the X-ray man at the pre-mother clinic had noticed two babies, though the sex, he had said, was a mystery.

Sade noticed Trudy's longing and put her hand down and said, Well, how does it feel to be having twins?

Trudy said, You get more accomplished than having

them one at a time. She said this as though she was talking about having one tooth extracted at a time as opposed to a whole mouthful.

My mother said, *Well, I hope you like boys then, because that's exactly what you're carrying. I took note of you walking from the rear and you seemed very squared off.*

Amanda and Sade had read girls, so Trudy was asked to walk again to break the tie. Trudy turned with her hands on what must have been a hurtful lower back and proceeded from one end of the store to the other one. Everybody looked with an eye towards sizing up sex.

When Trudy got to the door, she turned around and asked what they thought.

Then they all agreed and swore to Trudy that she was carrying a lapful of boys.

Trudy said, Good. She said, Boys' is all the names I've got.

Then she rounded up her children and started out. Amanda interrupted her leaving to ask what she planned to name the babies.

She told us, Bernard and Barnard, these names going so naturally together.

That fairly took our breath. My mother asked her

if that wouldn't get confusing, which it would.

Trudy said, No. She said she intended to call them Pee Wee and Buddy. Then she told us all to have a nice afternoon, and she organized her children out the door and walked the side of the road towards home.

We all got up a nickel or two and my mother trotted me out following Trudy and the children with a little sack of candy. After I caught up and handed over the bag, which they snatched, the children sat down on the ditchbank and fell into the sack. They ate it instantly and threw the bag in the ditch. Trudy picked it up and looked in it, threw it back down and pinched the oldest girl for not saving her any. I thought this was unusual for a mother to care so about candy, but Trudy had birthed first at thirteen and thus understandably mourned sweets.

When I got back to the rummy table, my mother had decided what to do about the Woodliefs. She told the women they'd donate money for Trudy's groceries, giving it directly to Porter and calling it credit. That way everybody would be pleased. We'd be helping, Porter would get his money, and Trudy's gang could eat without paying without stealing.

When Trudy returned and slammed her hand on the

counter, Porter said he could let her have a particular amount, whatever it was, fifty cents, a dollar, each week, no more no less.

She said in a curt manner, Damn! Ain't that swell?

But Trudy shopped that day and bought as much Cream of Wheat and Post Toasties as anyone had ever seen walk out of the store at once, thus inspiring in us all a great deal of hope for the Woodliefs.

Hope was dashed, though, the following week when my mother, in trying to get up a little community one-act something, approached the oldest Woodlief girl, Florence, about taking a small part, no talking or singing, just standing there. Everyone was eager to involve Florence, as she was so pretty and appeared so thoughtful. But Florence was of her own mind, and told my mother she didn't care to act in some goddamn homemade play. My mother's color left her. Goddamn simply rolled from the child. But Florence took the part finally for a nickel, a carpetbag full of dress-up clothes, and a generous bit of raw sugarcane.

9. *Of the father's distress,*
as well as that which he
caused others

"UNLIKE MY MOTHER AND ME, MY FATHER HAD no friends accumulated and thus had nowhere to sit but home when his work got slower and slower. Most mornings that he stayed at home, he and my mother fought two or even three times before breakfast. He mainly took issue with our habits.

He was frenzied by the sight of my mother and I waking up and taking out our rollers, dressing in something clean and pretty, though old, and heading out to take our constitutional. My mother used to scream and tell him we'd been going through the same motions since my hair was long enough to hold a curl, and he'd merely missed it.

You've worked, worked, worked. You've rarely seen Betty wake up and eat breakfast. And now you're here to witness our daily habits, which are none of your business and cost you nothing. We'll not stay in the house all day. You stay here! We're bored! And what's it costing you, anyway?

We weren't broke or destitute, though he told us that regularly. We certainly weren't in the shape of some we heard about, particularly families on the tramp between here and Washington who lived for days on flour and water gravy. And we hadn't been forced to sell our property to pay interest on our debts, as had the Bethunes. In spite of falling prices, the boll weevil, and his slowed gristmill business, my father was in as good if not better shape than anybody in our community, staying afloat in the main because he refused to borrow money, which may seem stern, and is, but piles of interest payments were onerous burdens.

My mother kept a fair accounting of how much money was coming through the house, although she advertised ignorance to my father in this regard. She knew if he said he had but fifty cents in his pocket, he had a dollar. She wasn't a mind-reader. She'd merely been listening to him and reading mail and cleaning out his pockets for nearly twenty years. Hearing as I have through life of men dying and leaving their wives knocked prostrate with the knowledge that their husbands drained their bank accounts, cashed in insurance policies, and plopped second mortgages on the house, I've wanted to ask these women, Where were your eyes? Did you never get to the mailbox first?

My father would repeat and repeat that his gristmill was going down, rocks and all, with Hoover. And then he'd swear that tomorrow would be the last day he'd have any work. The first ten or fifteen times we heard it we became upset because he seemed so overwrought, and my mother once got up and walked over behind his chair and put her arms around him. I certainly had never seen her touch him for any length of time without being brushed away and left embarrassed. She had learned to keep her hands to herself with him, which is, I'm sure, why she held my hand fairly continuously. So I was staggered by the sight of my mother showing her sympathy, but her intentions flew by him.

He began sounding like the boy who cried wolf. And then, after a month or so of listening to him, his supper table fears became more or less dentist office music. After a little longer, we even talked over his voice about the most trifling of things, like whether or not we should scallop a hemline that evening or whether or not Jack Benny was actually like he was on the air. My father seemed oblivious to anything but his own thoughts, but now I see this was the sign of him losing his reason.

He started up the ginning season of 1938 determined that he was going to make money hand over fist. He said as much. My mother would try to check his attitude. *Nobody has any money to pay you! This is not 1926! Did the boll weevil pack up and leave? Do you know something nobody else knows? I bet there're a hundred thousand farmers and ginners who'd like to know your secret plan for success this year.* Of course, this was considered none of my mother's business, so she got no answers.

But he certainly meant it when he said he was bound and determined to make money that season, and during the first week the mill was open he stunned everyone in the community by showing how little feeling he had for anybody but himself. Very simply, a boy working at the gin fell and was killed in the cotton baler, and after they got the boy out and had him taken away, my father ordered the others to clean up the equipment and crank everything back up to production. His employees were overcome by the ordeal and naturally asked to knock off for the afternoon, but my father threatened to fire them all and thus they worked.

My mother heard all this retold the day it happened by way of the boy's sister coming to our house and cursing my mother very severely. She gave the young woman money to count towards burial, which we were sure my father would refuse to provide. After the girl left, my mother laid dinner out on the table and sat very quietly waiting for my father to come home. I sat down with her quietly as well. I'd never heard her so quiet and still.

After he came in I waited for her to say something to him, maybe, *Anything interesting happen at work today?* But she didn't. She sat and watched him eating and then she got up and took her still full plate outside, and I eased away from the table and followed her. This probably made the thousandth time I'd trailed my mother from the table. All her life, when she rose, I rose.

She said to me in the yard, *Let's see if Woody and Bill are tied up.*

And then she put her hands to her mouth and whistled across the garden to our neighbor's two dogs, who came running like quarterhorses. These dogs hated everybody except their owners and my mother, I suppose because she'd made a great deal over them when they were small. But they were on the outs with the rest of humanity and had been known to jump completely through window glasses to get at drummers or the *Watch Tower* crowd or other people that they merely smelled or saw and wanted to bite.

My mother put the full plate down in the yard and Woody and Bill ate and ate and ate and then fairly smooched the plate when they were finished. But then right as they finished my father stomped out on the porch and lit into my mother for letting the dogs eat off his mother's dishes they'd carted all the way from Kentucky without breaking and on and on and on, I'd heard it a thousand times. The dogs stopped smacking their lips and stiffened and said, Grrr! Grrr! showing all their big teeth to my father. Then they more or less lunged for him. My father suddenly fell backwards into the house, like he'd been tied with a rope at the waist and yanked hard. Woody and Bill were very frustrated by the door, barking most ferociously. My father ran through the house and went out the back door and drove off in his automobile, I know with stars thrashing before his eyes.

Woody and Bill trotted over next to my mother's legs and she rubbed their heads and told them they could go back home. *You two can come back another time, if you don't mind. Betty and I have some dishes to wash.* They padded back across the garden, and later while my mother was putting a kettle on for dishwater, she smiled and told me without telling me how pleased she was with herself. *I'd forgotten how much those animals thought of me. I'd forgotten how much they dislike your father and how terrified he is of large dogs.*

This was the terrible start of a worse season. I remember hearing my mother tell Amanda how our lives would make such a good true story, the kind you hear on the radio, Ma Perkins and all the rest. Not long after that a man came through this part of the country selling Jerusalem beans and St. Jude roots for good luck. We all bought one of each.

IO. *Of the loss of the father to worry*

"MY FATHER BECAME LESS AND LESS ABLE TO manage his worries and concerns over money, restricting our household from top to bottom, adding something new daily to the list of things we couldn't have. My mother had recently learned to fish, and he all of a sudden denied her hooks. I had always loved licorice, and he said this was out as well. Nobody had ever starved over fish hooks and whip candy. We had such a hard time believing that he could be this concerned over literally a penny here and a penny there that we tried, in error, to chalk his anger up to his vision of us hanging off the side of the river bridge, with Polly Deal teaching us how to watch our bobbers.

And then there came another turn in the road! One Saturday morning my mother and I announced our desire to ride to town to window-shop, thinking my father would surely carry us and drop us off to do something so harmless. He wouldn't. He said he didn't want to part with the gasoline. He said we were both foolish. He said we acted and dressed and talked foolishly and we were lazy as well, and these things more or less added up to explain why he was saddled with supporting a seventeen-year-old daughter. He said if I was worth anything that I'd have long ago been spoken for. This was such a rude thing to say to a young girl. I'd have died for him to talk to me my entire life, and when he finally let go of more than a mumble, this is what came out.

That following Monday I followed an urge and mailed off and had two dresses sent to me on approval from the Butterick's ready-to-wear division. I simply couldn't help myself. Even my mother was huffy at first, but later that month when the beautiful dresses arrived and she saw how pretty they were, she placed an order through me. Then we both had our hands slapped.

My mother talked very fiercely to him.

This is your fault. You've brought this spree on yourself. All Betty and I had wanted to do was get out of the house to window-shop, but, oh boy, have we done more than window-shop now! I can't believe you've taken to hoarding gasoline from your own family, like we're forever asking to be carried somewhere. You act as if all Betty and I care to do is rip-roar up and down the highway gas-happy in your automobile. Haven't you ever seen or heard of us out walking? We together keep the weeds trampled down for miles up and down either side of Milk Farm Road!

He listened and walked out. Anger was called for in return, but he was numb past the point of being able to rally. While he was gone, my mother and I discussed the matter and decided to tell him that evening that we would send the dresses back to Butterick's. However, we didn't return the dresses. We sold them to Amanda Bethune for less than half price, on time, and we loaned her the money to make the payments. This way we still could enjoy looking at them and everyone was more or less pleased.

Two weeks later my father left the house early, dressed so as my mother believed he was headed to town on business. He didn't act unnatural or unusual in any way at all, but then he didn't come home and he didn't come home. And then the next morning he was spotted wedged between two big rocks down in the bend of the river.

My mother was so mad at him that she didn't want him laid out in the house. *Does he think he can do this and then enjoy the living room? He'll go directly into the ground.*

I convinced her that we couldn't do that. It wasn't done. I told her that trying to punish a dead person was futile. She would have to write what was left of his family and give them the chance to come or not come. We actually had to move right along, though, as he was already at the point that Polly Deal could hardly button his vest. This seemed to make my mother madder.

She refused to play hostess, so I had to. She sat stiffly in a ladderback chair with her arms crossed and both feet flat on the floor during the entire ordeal, wearing the disputed print which Amanda had given back to her. Women tried to tell her she looked pretty in the cotton print, but she repelled each compliment in the same manner my father had brushed her arms and hands from him all those years. All she would take was Polly's tea.

My thoughts on this have hardened over time. I understand that many, many men took their lives during those years, and if my father had lost a corporation in a tumble to the soup line, I could see thoughts of starving workers and families driving him to self-destruction. But he was a very simple man with a very simple farm and side-business, and a very simple wife and child. He merely glorified everything in light of his family history and his pushing urge to thrive. He killed himself solely for himself, and it was, in his case, a more particularly selfish act than usual. He didn't die for fear of failure in our eyes. He was not at all of this mind. If he'd been able to work, work, work without cease as always, I'm sure he would've lived on and died in a field or at his mill, thinking he'd lived a perfectly sane life.

The minute my mother and I were over our shock we sat down and unscrambled our thoughts and said, What do we do? Of course, right away was the matter of insurance. My father being found in the river in his Sundayest clothes was suspicious from the start and thus neither his life nor burial policies paid out. If he'd not worn a suit and if he had been thoughtful enough to take some bait and tackle to the river with him, our financial consequences would have come out on the upswing. This was just one more thing my mother chalked up against him and Herbert Hoover. The one relief was the appearance one morning of Gordon Randolph, who said he wanted to rent our acreage plus the mill. My mother and I, who'd never really concerned ourselves in this regard, said, Do it! Take it! Fine!

Not long after this, Odessa Hightower, the public health nurse who had started the pre-mother clinics that kept up with Trudy and many, many other young women, also appeared with good news. However, it was good news my mother and I didn't actually need, but we didn't refuse, either, on grounds that my father had paid taxes galore. Here was Odessa with news that my mother automatically qualified for a small bit of widow's aid, despite the suspicious circumstances. And she also bore food, a huge brick of government cheese and a beautiful roast beef, which we sliced and enjoyed that very night. I had felt like it all along, but that's when I knew that Mr. Roosevelt had the love of God in his heart.

My mother and I were forced to take a very steely attitude about the suicide in relation to what people wanted to know and expected to be told. Louise Miracle visited our home, and while my mother was in the kitchen getting something, Louise whispered, wanting to know how my father was found. She apologized for having to ask this, which was actually farther than even my mother usually tended to go with anybody's business.

I told her, How do I know? I wasn't there! How do I know?

My mother heard this coming back into the room, and she sat down and took my hand and proceeded to surprise our company. *Charles was discovered upside down, straight upside down on his head with the river rocks on either side, like bookends.*

When Louise left, which was in fairly no time at all, my mother told me that more often than not people will not be satisfied until they've heard what they want to hear. She also said that all the curiosity seeking would stop as soon as the community had a fresh tragedy to attend to. Thank goodness we had another one very soon when a man of unknown origin laid down in front of the train. We enjoyed the idea of Louise Miracle down by the tracks, asking questions of the conductor. This event worked the trick in taking the community's mind off my father in spite of the fact this man was simply a rover of the sort that supposedly shot Roy Duplin. But still, curiosities shifted and my mother and I went back about our business.

II. *An account of welcome new life on Milk Farm Road*

"WHERE THERE'S DEATH, THERE'S LIFE, AND though with nothing ready for the babies but a set of fancy names, Trudy had her twins, and they were boys. The entire community stepped in with food and offers to clean, although my mother and I decided that most of the women involved simply wanted a good look at the inside of Trudy's house. They thought her belongings would be strange or unusual in some respect because of Louisiana.

I went to visit the babies as soon as Polly would let them be viewed. Polly had caught them, even though she'd threatened to leave Trudy hanging. She distrusted Trudy to pay her and in the end my mother gave Polly the ten-dollar fee in case Trudy balked at the bill, which she did. The babies needed a boost, so Polly arranged for Odessa Hightower to bring the pink warmer with the pretty hatching Easter egg pictures on the ends instead of the usual white one, which Polly had seen many young women resist because of its coffiny look. Polly Deal was very wise with women.

My interest was perked for babies, for reasons I was blind to at the time. I'm sure that motherly feelings were sparked in my mind because of the Dionne quints and all their radio uproar and publicity, notwithstanding the fact that I was eighteen with no view to the altar.

When I arrived at the Woodliefs, Florence let me in and led me into the kitchen to Trudy, who was already up and around on her feet on day ten in size six street clothes. She had dropped her baby weight immediately, which was somewhat of a miracle. I commented that I'd come to see the babies and made kind remarks about her looks, to which she responded that she liked to slough off baby weight right away.

Her secret was to live on cigarettes until she could button her old clothes and then she'd switch back to normal food. I knew this wasn't safe and told her so. She said, I might get weak-headed, but I'd rather see spots than carry weight. She told me several times that she wasn't going to lose her figure, and she also said she regretted to hear about my father, which surprised me. She said she'd have gone to the wake but failed to get everything moving in the right direction to get out of the house that day. Then she returned to mixing a big quart of the babies' bottle formula. She didn't nurse because she was afraid that nursing one baby right after another one would give her cancer, and besides, nursing wasn't in trend in our community, going in and out as it does in waves.

I asked Trudy where the little boys were and she told me they were both in a bedroom resting in the warmer and that I was welcome to look as long as I didn't wake them up. She said she'd gone through hell to get them both asleep.

I looked in and saw them there asleep so beautifully, sleeping both alike, with their fists by their ears. I knew twins were small, but I just thought these were smaller than usual. Actually, they were very wizzled up and the size of wolf-rats. How much had they weighed at birth?

She told me, Four something apiece. She told me she was used to having pre-born babies, all very slight, putting two fingers out in front of her like she was describing a trout.

I saw something like a cigar box attached to the far end of the warmer. What's that?

Trudy told me to go look at it. It actually was a cigar box, and it was open with a little message written inside the lid that went: GIVE TO THE TRIBUTES IN THE NAME OF JESUS.

Trudy had pulled the verse out of midair but it sounded so thoroughly Biblical that surely not many were the wiser. And the babies had collected sixty cents to show for it, so it actually didn't matter. I had never heard of this manner of charity, but Trudy said that was the way things were done in Louisiana. She also said it was human nature to associate all babies with baby Jesus, even two at one time, so she was just allowing her company to please God through her twins, and so everybody was happy.

Odessa Hightower had stopped by earlier to okay the babies and the warmer, although Trudy felt she'd visited to merely criticize her children's fingernails. Odessa impressed Trudy as a big rambler in affairs, having something haughty to say about her manner of collection.

I liked agreeing with Trudy. I liked the way it felt. So I said that the nurse was full of her position or something of that nature, and Trudy boomed at me, Tell it!

This woke up the babies and they just cried like, well, they cried like babies. I told her I'd love to get the boys back to sleep, although I could not have told her how I intended to do it.

Don't you know she was glad for a break? She went back to her other children and I picked up both babies and rocked and hummed and rocked and hummed them right on back to sleep, curled in my arms. They slept like little men.

12. *A clash of stubborn wills*

"Soon I was absorbed with Trudy Woodlief and her situation. I helped convince Gordon Randolph to let her keep the house for a song, and I inspired her to study the first leg of the Gregg course to prepare her, as my mother said, for a brighter day. I knew what she believed about the world, having sat with her many evenings praising Mr. Roosevelt, who we all worshiped all his twelve years, one month, and eight days in office. People can say what they will of Trudy's mothering, but she rocked her children in the Democratic cradle.

My mother softened and softened on Trudy to the point

that she several times invited the children to our home for precious coconut cake, eventually learning to suffer ingratitude. Many times we'd look out of our door and see a clump of children waiting to eat cake when they should've been in school, which they attended in fits and starts. I simply can't name all their names, which are jumbled up with the exceptions of Florence and Barnard and also Bernard, whom my mother refused to call Pee Wee and Buddy.

The children weren't unschooled from lack of shoes and clothes, though these things were lacking. Trudy simply fell into the sticks getting them all up and dressed in the morning, and even something as easy as throwing a sweet potato into a lunch bucket was a trial for her. She woke up every morning behind from the night before. She performed miracles, by my estimation, surviving days, notwithstanding the fact that she openly refused to knock herself out to the extent of most other rural mothers.

Clean clothes being the greatest obstacle for Trudy, my mother decided that I'd collect their clothes, bring them to our house and help Polly Deal wash and hang the things out, and then cart them back down the hill when they eventually dried. Of course, this was not Polly Deal's pleasure, but we slipped her additional wages and thus she obliged us.

We didn't fold, however. We left this for the children as my mother and Polly said this would build their character. But they folded in such a slaphappy manner that I'm sure no progress was made regarding their moral fiber. And then once the clothes were folded, such as they were, there were no drawers to put them in, so they sat around waiting to get dirty on the floor, in corners, all of which was not acceptable to my mother. Thus she sent downhill my father's chest of drawers, a beautiful piece which had come in the wagon from Kentucky, which Trudy used primarily for stacking clothes on, not in, until the twins came out of the warmer looking for somewhere to sleep. Trudy never said to me, I hope you don't mind me using these beautiful deep oak drawers as baby beds. When my mother asked me one day how the dresser was working out for the Woodliefs I told her, Fine. And, of course, she acted miffed that I couldn't say more.

Once I was sitting in Trudy's kitchen watching her children ball up clothes and throw them on the chest, and I asked her in a nice way if she thought she would have any more children when she had the difficulty she did taking care of the ones she had.

She told me not without a husband. Then she asked if I knew what was the best thing about a man cutting the line.

I pretended that there could be no joy in a man's leaving. But Trudy said, Yes it is. You don't have to worry over coming down with another baby.

Thus she meant that if she was married she couldn't help herself from having babies. I told her that she didn't necessarily have to keep creating new life upon new life. In so many words, if you don't want butter you can pull the dasher out.

She became very haughty and said, I've had seven children. I reckon I know what I'm doing, thank you.

I didn't think she knew what she was doing, having sat and watched her grease the new babies' knees with dishwater to make them walk sooner. As well, she'd shown my mother and I an ugly case of the babies' thrush, which she proclaimed to be curing by letting horses blow in their mouths.

My mother shouted out loud, *Do not do that! I'll give you something in a tube! Do not do that!* The health crowd

94

also did not believe Trudy knew what she was doing. After hearing from my mother concerning the dishwater and horses' breath and what have you, Odessa Hightower carried her vaccination campaign to the Woodlief children, who of course rejected the needle.

We'd all taken shots in the arm the first day Odessa came around announcing her germ war. In fact, she appeared at the store and went from arm to arm around the rummy table. Although some took the shots out of healthful concern, others consented because Odessa could be so unctuous in this regard. Very superior. I'm sure when she died and entered heaven she asked to see the upstairs. She had a particular manner that made women feel unclean whether we had soaked all morning or merely washed in spots. On the day she gave her shots, she opened her satchel and tried to pass out tooth powders, talcum, and little nail brushes, stunning everyone, particularly the women who had made a life of grooming their families. She said something like, I can't stress enough the importance of clean fingernails. But she had the vaccine, so everyone bore her and prayed that once the hardship was over that Mr. Roosevelt would see his way clear to take her out of the field.

Then, while I was away in town one afternoon, Odessa

convinced my mother to go down the hill with her and talk Trudy into protecting her children, and thus it was through Odessa that my mother saw the chest of drawers piled with balled-up clothing and the drawers sprawled out of place full of babies. I was very happy not to have been with my mother at this time.

Trudy finally was scared into making her children sit for shots, Odessa and my mother having oppressed her into feeling very, very unfit had she refused again. And so while Trudy held child after child in her lap for Odessa, my mother unballed and folded the laundry and regarded the entire bedding situation of all these children.

That afternoon when I got home I saw two colored men bringing my beautiful mahogany baby bed piece by piece out of the attic with my mother telling them how not to bump it. They brought down as well a wool rug we had bought on a whim and gotten home only to have it match nothing, mocha brown with wisps and sprays of crabapple over it.

Then my mother filled my pockets with ten-penny nails and handed me the hammer and told me to follow the men down the hill and create places for the Woodliefs to hang their clothes. I was concerned, and told her I was concerned, about going into a home and putting holes in the wall. But my mother said I had a perfect right to do this. *Anytime somebody's not looking after themselves it becomes your business.*

So I went and did it, after having asked Trudy if she wouldn't like to have what amounted to fresh closet space, to which she replied she couldn't give a damn and to nail if I felt like nailing. I later lied, telling my mother that Trudy expressed her warm appreciation for both the baby bed and the hanging places.

She glared at me and yelled, *Phooey.*

There was simply no point, I suppose, in lying to my mother about this or any other disappointment in human nature. Like Polly Deal, my mother was also very, very wise with people.

13. *Of the mother*
and daughter's curious
excursion from
Milk Farm Road, with
a full account of the
Irish calamity

"MY MOTHER WAS BLUNT WITH WOMEN WHO wanted to know her plans for the future. She always knew what they meant. *You mean what am I going to do about finding another man? Well, I've been married enough.*

She often reminded them that World War I had torn up the community to the extent that a search for an unmarried man her age with two arms, two hands, two legs, and half a brain intact would be thoroughly futile. But this wasn't so. This is merely what she remarked in public.

And then I formed the idea that my mother and I should

go away and live elsewhere. But she wouldn't leave the community, even though I knew that if we moved somewhere bigger, one or the both of us would find a nice man and be married within a year. She told me this was impossible in regard to her. *If I'm supposed to marry again, whoever wants me will have to come to Milk Farm Road and find me.* This happening, by 1938, was the true impossibility.

I asked her, Why would anyone come?

There's the nice little store and the nice people and the nice pace to daily living. It's not Richmond, Virginia, but it's not Bell County, Kentucky, either.

I then saw my mother looking back on her life and seeing how far she had come since she and her family clawed to hang onto the bottom rung. On Milk Farm Road she'd remade herself into the Queen Bee, more or less organizing life through knowing everything. Anywhere else she'd be one of the crowd. Her dresses wouldn't have been as impressive and neither would her intellect. She'd taken her chance once and wouldn't risk leaving her home another time.

I've already left my home and people I love one time. I'll not do it again.

It seemed to me that she had enjoyed taking her turn, and now she expected me to do without mine, and of course this had to feel unfair. And then I began to see everything around me differently from her, which was a change very late in coming. So late, in fact, that I know my mother had given up on it, believing independence had peeked up once in my refusal to eat healthful foods but then vanished again. I teamed up with her against my father so much that she mistook my companionship for a lack of free will. And then once he was dead and I asked her for my liberty, finally, she simply couldn't understand me.

I looked around at my home. The store, though nice, was still small. And the people, though nice, had aged by leaps during the Depression, and their children, the ones my age, were married and involved with their families. My mother and I soon started to fight, and we fought all summer. I was desperate to get out of our community before it locked up to crumble in on itself.

I asked Trudy what she'd do if she were me. She said I was smart and pretty and could talk and would thus fare well anywhere. She, in fact, had moved and lived all over, heading from place to place beating rent. One choice she suggested was New York, which I balked at as too out-landish. Trudy, however, had been there several times visiting Tommy's people and reported liking everything about it except for the noise, the dirt, and the people. I continued to resist New York and said that with this one exception I could actually see the world as open to me.

But then there came another turn in the road! A chance fell upon my mother and me to leave the community though just for a while. She hoped this would satisfy my urge, but I couldn't promise her it would or it wouldn't.

The particular event was my grandmother Bridget O'Cadhain's strong urge to die. She had woken up one morning in Bell County, Kentucky, yearning to return to Ireland and pass, all brought on by dreams of angels and muddy water and visions of coffins in candles. My mother's sisters wrote her with news of Bridget's desire and said the old woman, very old, had harassed them all and even threatened to throw their children in the well if someone didn't step forth to take her back to Ireland.

They all knew that Bridget was not beneath telling false tales in this regard. They knew she hadn't really seen her death. She had, however, craved Galway for fifty years and had hatched many dashed plans to go. This time she was determined, and she backed her ears and went at getting to Galway and promised no peace in the household until someone agreed to take her. She'd counted on Sheamus to take her in 1928 but was disappointed by his death that same year. My mother had received the dark news on a penny postcard that said:

> Papa came in and had fresh shad for supper and said he felt fine but then late in the night he dropped dead. Sincerely Eileen.

This note impressed my mother as odd, and everytime we'd see the postcard in our album she would find her queer look and comment on how the strange note was so in keeping with her family.

The arrangements for the Irish trip were made behind our backs. One of the sisters fixed Bridget with the idea that my mother still owed her from 1918 and thus she should escort her. Understandably, the thought of accompanying the old woman appealed to no one. And then Bridget decided that this plan was fair and true and thus she put all her faith in my mother to come and carry her. All this broke my mother's heart to the point that she talked to the bank, and off we went to Bell County. I was to stay in Kentucky while my mother and Bridget went away.

Of course Bridget couldn't afford the trip. Mr. Hoover had been especially rough on Kentucky. But she accumulated more than enough money for her passage. She had gone to each of the children, there were ten, and humiliated them to the point that they sold animals and automobiles and whatever they could find to sell to give their mother money. One son sold half his timber land. She made them feel guilty over not having enough children, not looking after her in her old age, not speaking Gaelic.

The journey was beautiful and green. I remember I sat on the train by my mother and held a hatbox full of cape jasmines in my lap. She had them packed in wet cotton and covered them with a fabric. Her sisters loved cape jasmines and had been denied them by their weather so we promised to take them some, more or less as my mother's peace offering. She was very eager to get home, although the coming questions about my father alarmed her, I could tell.

The O'Cadhain house was a sight, painted in a very spotty fashion, though certainly as large a home as I'd ever experienced. When children married they stayed and threw rooms onto the house as necessary and thus the whole place was continuously changing and growing, fairly in motion over the side of the hill. My first impression of my mother's family was startling. These were the kind of people who crack nuts in the house and leave the hulls on the floor. At all turns, their social edge seemed to be lacking. As much as my mother had advised me to dress simply, I of course outdressed my aunts and cousins and nieces, all of whom twisted my sleeve, wanting to know when they could try my dress on. Eileen, I noticed right away, was wearing two dresses, as later I discovered she did every day, an old one on top to protect the better one underneath. This is the sort of oddity I faced even as I came through the door.

Bridget was exactly as in my mind's eye, down to the nubby teeth, though by 1938 she had lost most of her teeth to pull taffy, as had most of her family. She walked through, not into, the room right after my mother and I arrived and pursed her lips at us and hobbled away. She was almost eighty then so thus her trademark of trotting had slowed considerably. My mother watched Bridget leave the room needless to say without hopping up to create a beautiful reunion. She looked more or less pained.

As soon as we were out of our traveling frocks, we were put to work sweeping and tending to babies and barely regarded as company. Four or five days were to pass before my mother and Bridget left for Ireland, and during this time we were both ignored as guests and treated as chambermaids, for truth. I frankly think that with so many people in the house, they simply lost count from time to time and forgot we were there. My discomfort reared up in a sweaty nightmare that I became trapped there, made to hang out diapers, and everytime I thought the basket was empty a thousand more baby diapers appeared, like the loaves and the fishes.

On the last night before my mother left with Bridget, one of her sisters asked in a very huffy manner exactly how my father had died. My mother had staved off this question, it seemed, for as long as she could, but the time had finally come to answer it.

She lost herself in her plate, to keep her eyes from glancing to me, and told a very moving account of how my father pulled a rover from in front of a train, thus sparing the hobo's life and losing his own. She actually tuned up and whimpered and then recited a little tribute the rover made at my father's service.

This was a very wonderful point in my life, even more so when my aunts shouted, Oh, we've judged him wrong! Oh, his blessed soul! However, as sorry as they felt for my mother and me, they still stuck us with a tubful of dishes while they all played whist.

Although Bridget wanted her family to believe they'd never see her again, she barely winced upon leaving. I'd made a bigger deal over leaving Trudy Woodlief. I was very reluctant to see my mother go, not to mention the fact that I'd be shut up in a house with more or less fifty strangers. We'd not been separated an evening. She looked very pretty and pulled together for the trip in spite of the fact that Bridget, once out of the door for the train station, walked along behind my mother, nipping at her in her black.

After they left I explored all around the area with the intention of finding my father's roots. His family that had settled in Bell County had picked up eventually and roved to parts unknown in Tennessee, so when I finally asked and asked about in the little Quaker area, all I was directed to was a cemetery.

All my life I'd heard my father remark that his mother had been a very strong believer in salvation by grace and that she had led her community's pacifist movement and suffered ridicule greatly during World War I. She sounded very progressive in her thinking, though still firm in her church. And I featured her with a calm nature and a gentle disposition and I many times wished I'd known her. My mother, however, told me that the woman was actually surly, that she had a dark outlook, never smiled, and couldn't cook. That was as much as she ever said about my father's family.

Once I found the woman's stone, I stood and stood and tried to feel either joy that she had been my grandmother or sorrow that she was dead. But all I could do was read her stone and wonder how they afforded it, it was large and beautiful, and what possessed someone to write that they marvel in the finished work of the Lord. We marvel in the finished work of the Lord.

My mother, in the meantime, was involved in Bridget's difficulties, riding sick and embarrassed all the way across the Atlantic Ocean. Bridget drew notice everywhere. No doubt my mother was passing at acting as if she knew what she was doing, standing in this or that line, tipping correctly, as suggested by her reading. But the minute Bridget stuck my mother in the back with her cane and snapped at her in Gaelic, my mother's ease was flung into the ocean.

Your grandmother made me miserable. I couldn't understand her and I'd become nervous, which seemed to thrill her because she'd push at me stronger. But though I can't say she would've cried had I fallen overboard, I also can't say she was a bad woman. She'd hardened herself to live with my father, and this would've made the best of us mean-spirited. I have difficulty judging her, although she had no difficulty tormenting me trapped on the boat with her.

Once they arrived at Galway, Bridget insisted on being taxied from Cork to Galway simply because she'd never ridden in a taxicab. Then once they got to Galway and found the little thatched roof O'Donough house, Bridget entered without knocking and barked at the man of the house to go pay the driver.

My mother assumed her sisters had notified these relatives of the visit, but of course they hadn't, thus more frustration. She apologized and apologized and set herself to organizing their arrangements, then Bridget started sending the children out into the neighborhood to collect women for the death watch.

The O'Donough woman said, A nice visit we can do, but none of this.

But in the end she lost her will to Bridget and the ladies came and were paid and arranged themselves in chairs in the wide hall by Bridget's door. Not saying a word to anyone, Bridget went and crawled in the bed with her head towards the west. My mother was so humiliated by all this that she left the house.

I walked and walked in the night-cool and came to a pretty little inn type of place and went inside and ate the most of an entire loaf of soda bread. I sat with the baker, who made me guess the ingredients, which took my mind off my mother's insanity. However, I had to return to the three women crying and the O'Donough couple shuffling around the house still very confused over our coming. I went in their bedroom, which my mother had assumed for her own, and saw her there sleeping, curled on the bed, snoring and drooling away, still in her dress.

Out of the house I carried myself, back to the soda bread inn. I took a room and stayed there all night. When I returned in the morning I walked towards an uproar in the kitchen, and there stood my mother screaming and waving her fists at the household, yelling how ill-mannered they were not to have a nice breakfast prepared for her. She jabbed her cane at them and said she was leaving to go stay with old Mrs. So-and-So, who would treat her better, but the cousins said this lady was dead. Bridget said, Fine, then I'll go stay with another old So-and-So. And she was dead too. She named off five or six people and they were all long dead, and then she whirled around and blamed me for dragging her off to Ireland to visit a bunch of dead people.

So thus my grandmother had fallen asleep dying. But at least she had gone back to Ireland. On the way back to Kentucky my mother had quite a time continuously making up tales for ticket people concerning Bridget's one-way accommodations, which had been so foolishly bought before. But they finally returned, and I was thrilled and relieved to see my mother, aged as she seemed though in the face.

Bridget O'Cadhain outlived most everybody she had ever known. At ninety-seven she tripped in the yard with a bucket, thus breaking bones that by nature would never knit. She was placed on a cot in the kitchen and ran the household from this corner. And from all reports, when she finally died, she very unwillingly went.

14.

Of Betty's decision to seek her happiness in Virginia and what happened to her on the way

"MY TRIP TO KENTUCKY PACIFIED MY URGE, as my mother had hoped and predicted, but only for a while. After we returned home, whenever I mentioned wanting to go somewhere my mother would say, *You just got back from somewhere and already you're talking about going again!* I was made to feel childish, like I'd just eaten a beautiful dessert and was already hungry for another one. So I was even more frustrated. Trudy, though lacking in high ideals, was realistic with her very practical nature, so I went to her for answers.

I said, Trudy, I feel so hemmed in here. I feel like

I'm less and less marriageable as day after day passes.

She told me the only way I would be happy on Milk Farm Road with my mother would be to turn off the radio. This would eliminate a great deal of temptation.

Then she said I should do what I wanted to do or give up and fall into having babies, or at least for her sake stop whining. She said that before her eyes I was turning into a moping whiner.

Soon after this, sitting by my mother at cards, she reached out and took one of my hands and rubbed and played with it, as she had always done when she was trying hard to think of what card to play next. I took my hand back and announced to the group that I was thinking about moving—to where, I didn't know.

I felt a great deal of power saying this. My mother licked her finger and tossed out a card and told me to send her a penny postcard. I was appalled at her for being so slick. I left and went home to try and figure out how to manage my happiness, which was difficult as feeling guilty and hopeful at the same time is more or less undoable.

But once I had it in my mind to leave, I worked towards this end, sending off for schools and work programs in the mail and what-have-you. I finally decided to go to Richmond and work-study through a W.P.A. commercial course that I believed would stand me in good stead for the rest of my life.

Although I'd completed all my high school plus two Gregg courses, I certainly had no prospects of working on Milk Farm Road, as there simply wasn't a great call for typing and steno in our community. Women either received aid or worked beside their husbands, or like my mother, of all people, depended on the man for income. This was all and this was it. So, I believed that once I completed the W.P.A. course in Richmond I'd be more or less too educated to return home and find any sort of fulfillment on Milk Farm Road.

I managed to convince Polly Deal to move in the house with my mother while I was away. Then I walked downhill and told Trudy I was taking her advice on doing what I wanted to do and pleasing myself. But all this fell on deaf ears, as it were, as she'd already forgotten having the conversation. With all that many children, so much had happened to her between then and now. But she seemed happy for me, although I had to assure her several times that the laundry bonanza wouldn't stop when I left. And of course the children demanded to be sent pretty things.

The day before I left I polled women at the store to see who could walk me through riding the train alone. Amanda Bethune knew the process thoroughly and told me exactly what I'd see and what to do even after I arrived in Richmond. My mother jumped in and said that everything Amanda described may've been rearranged or torn down since her visit.

How do you know that the canteen is still on the right side of the building through the door under the big clock? Things change. Everything changes. Suppose they fired the nice lady at the ticket counter? Suppose Richmond rearranged the bus stops? Everything changes.

She wanted me to say, Yes, I'll probably get lost and look foolish. The risk is so great I'll stay home. But I couldn't, even though every night when I'd close my eyes I'd see myself lost in downtown Richmond, wandering with my mouth open and of course in danger.

My first incident away from home fairly rattled me to the point that I considered getting off the train in Roanoke Rapids and turning around and going back home to my mother. It dealt with her hatbox.

While I was packing my things, my mother had come in and given me a pair of patents that hurt her feet and her hatbox, the one she'd packed with cape jasmines for Kentucky. I told her I wasn't going to take her good hat and I had no desire for cape jasmines, although I'd certainly be thrilled with the shoes. And then she shook her head and made her business known.

Good luck with the shoes, but I wouldn't give you my nice hat to ruin handling by the brim. No sir. And Virginia is full of flowers. The hatbox is empty. Pack it lightly or carry it empty if you wish, but you'll need to carry a hatbox. It's the mark of a lady to carry a hatbox traveling. All the way to Kentucky you thought you were merely a girl riding beside her mother, but this certainly wasn't the way others saw you. You appeared as a young lady with a hat too nice to ride with the suit satchels overhead.

I asked her how she knew this about ladies and hatboxes and trains. She told me she'd heard it. That's it. *I heard it.* Then she put the hatbox on my bed and left. I looked at it a while, loving the sight of me carrying it and this time understanding everything it meant. I wouldn't carry it empty, though. I decided to pack it with light underthings. It would be difficult otherwise, I thought, to walk about and pretend the box was weighted. The flowers had been perfect.

So there I sat on the train holding the hatbox on my lap, trying to look like a lady and to do so naturally. I'll have to say I looked nice, well pulled together. I had very trim hips at this point and had chosen something on the clingy though sophisticated side for the trip. My hair was perfectly waved as well, clasped on the side with the faux ruby barrette, which I'd more or less stolen from my mother's vanity cache. I tried to keep everyone's attention off of my hands. I had sat at home debating for hours over whether or not to paint my nails, which I had just lately learned not to chew. My mother advised me that nothing looked as cheap as cheap nail polish, which was all I had, so off I went to Richmond, Virginia, with bare nails.

I could sense women inspecting me and and eyeing the hatbox and classing me a few rungs higher than I belonged. I thus felt my confidence rising. I thought about how right my mother had been, even though I hadn't been thoroughly convinced that fooling a trainload of strangers was honorable or even necessary. But by the time we got to Weldon I was nearly squealing, realizing that striking airs might not be honorable but it would certainly attract a higher class of young man than Luther Miracle. And by the time we crossed the state line I had worked myself into such a state over my coming new life that I'd bitten off one hand of nails without thinking and was about to start on the next. I caught notice of myself and gently placed both hands back down, as ladies wouldn't chew a nail in public, hatbox or no hatbox.

So there I was, trying to regain my poise, and a lady said, Excuse me, but I can't help but notice the brand of hat you're carrying. I happen to do a little millinery work when I can and I'd just love to see your hat.

I told her I'd rather not, but she continued to press me to the point that I was afraid she would come over and jerk the box from me and open the lid. I squeezed the box to me and tried to smile firmly.

I said, Listen, if I showed you this hat you'd want to buy it from me and I happen to be very attached to this one particular hat.

She said, Heavens no! I just want a little look!

Then she got up and started moving towards me and I was frightened out of my wits. I'd never seen a woman so determined to see a hat. All in the world I could see at that moment was that curious milliner coming towards me. I jumped up and more or less whizzed past her and went and sat in another compartment, and I rode the rest of the way to Richmond terrified that I'd feel a tap on my shoulder and hear, Just one little peek at your hat? However, I knew the woman was occupied with all the other women laughing at me. Even though all I could hear was rumble, rumble, rumble, I'd spent enough time around women to know what they considered funny, and it certainly included the likes of me posing as a lady for a handful of strangers on a train. And thus I arrived in Richmond as myself.

15. *An account of Betty's Richmond education, with several other events worth notice, not the least of which would be Polly Deal's traumatic handkerchief episode*

"I MOVED INTO A ROOMING HOUSE SET ASIDE FOR the young girls taking this particular commercial course. During the early morning hours I attended very drab classes, by my estimation, and then practiced typing and dictation until noon. Then I ate lunch and went to the job Mr. Roosevelt's crowd had found for me as a way of earning towards my tuition. They'd assigned me to clerk in a candy kitchen. This, to sum it up, was not my pleasure.

Soon, however, I met a girl with some pull who got me on Saturdays at Kresge's. You really had to have pull to get any of the advantages. I liked Kresge's a great deal. My mother was more pleased with me there, and I kept her rummy players and Polly in pretty though modest gloves and handkerchiefs.

As well, I saved and bought gifts for the Woodliefs, my mother, and myself. For the children, of course, toys. For Trudy, a beautiful repossessed Mixmaster, which my mother and Polly walked downhill and taught her to use and which she used frequently, to everyone's surprise. For my mother, a clock which played the "Emperor Waltz" and apparently ground on Polly's nerves incessantly. For me, a tiny marcasite pin.

I socialized, as had always been my nature, with older women, longtime Kresge's employees as well as my secretarial instructors. In the main all these women had been raised in Richmond. Nothing much turned their heads. Through these friends, as a matter or fact, I learned how to drink Earl Grey tea with milk, which was rough at first but by sheer force of habit became something I love.

I enjoyed meeting the nice class of people who traded at Kresge's, particularly one very good-looking young man, Stanton, who frequented my register and seemed to have all kinds of money to spend. He bought a great deal of toiletries, and I was amazed at all the little daily grooming neccessities other Americans were doing without that he bought continuously. People just didn't spend money on three shades of shoe polish, but Stanton did. He had a lovely overcoat as well.

I'd heard that working near the law offices I'd sooner or later meet somebody who was more or less a Virginia gentleman. Although Stanton ended up not actually coming from money, he drew a pretty good check, and in 1939 a young girl like myself rarely split hairs. And although I had never spent much time at all around young men, I seemed to do everything right when it came to drawing Stanton's attentions. At first I thought his job and money and the mere fact of him living in Richmond would make him simply look twice and walk on, but it didn't.

In no time at all Stanton and I hooked up and all we did was go. We went all the time! Though I didn't drink —I never liked the way it tasted—I kept the same long hours and wild pace of those who did. Some nights Stanton and I attended house parties given by the university set, and on slow nights we spent evenings playing whist and bridge or trying to make the spirits rap. A highlight was going with him and several other young people to see the Skating Vanities, which I thought was wonderful fun and made everyone yearn to skate.

On several weekends I'd pretend to be headed home and then off Stanton and I would go, usually up over by the Eastern Shore to various nice homes owned by the free and easy crowd. All night parties were the rule there, with a great deal of sneaking off and coming back in. By the time the sun rose I was usually the only one sober as well as the only young girl who'd kept to herself, though this isn't to say that Stanton never tried to maul me.

My health started going downhill and in no time at all Stanton put me on pep pills. He seemed to have this sort of medication at his disposal, though at the time the fact that he kept pep pills in his pockets like loose change didn't alarm me as it should've. Next came the female regulators to even out my emotions, which seemed to rotate continuously.

I was taking so much of this and that to study and work that I attempted to put myself to sleep nights with a tall glass of Ovaltine, which was the rage. Stanton swore by Ovaltine and guaranteed it would knock me out but I swear I think it jiggled up my pep even more. I soon received a warning for not always showing up at school precisely, and thus I eased off the Ovaltine as well as the regulators, which testifies to the fact that I wasn't hooked.

Three entire months went by without a visit home, and I really started to feel anxious about wanting to see my mother. We wrote frequently but of course this is never the same. So, one Sunday morning Stanton and I hopped in his car and headed south. I was very nervous though proud to be coming home with a sport. My mother's opinion was still very important, in spite of my new independence.

We drove in the yard and walked up the steps into the house, and so far things seemed to be going very smoothly. Then my mother came in and we hugged and so on, and then I introduced her to Stanton. We small-talked a bit about the yard and such and about Polly, who my mother said had been jerked away from the breakfast table to catch a baby.

As we talked, I noticed my mother couldn't keep her eyes off Stanton. I assumed she looked at him as hard as she did because he was so good-looking, and it didn't seem to faze him at all as he was used to being goggled at by women. She told him to make himself comfortable, that she needed to borrow me a minute. She grabbed me under the elbow and fairly lifted me into the kitchen.

When we were by ourselves, she said she had a few questions.

I said, Like what?

Like why are that boy's lips blue?

I said, What?

Why are they blue? Polly and I soaked cotton stockings in indigo last week and aimed for such a blue. They're unnatural, Betty.

At first I thought it was just my mother noticing details, but when I went back in the room and saw him there on the sofa, the sight sunk in. I don't know how I could've been so blind. Perhaps they'd been turning so slowly I hadn't noticed, like plants growing. But, yes, they were blue. I tried not to say anything and enjoy lunch and the afternoon, but once I noticed Stanton's lips, when I looked at him they were all I could see. I could tell they were driving my mother crazy. I would see her catch herself staring at them and glance off, but then she finally gave up and simply locked her gaze.

I welcomed the relief of Stanton saying he wanted to walk out and enjoy the grape arbor while my mother and I caught up. She and I spent the entire time he was out of the house arguing.

They're certainly blue all right, like he's frozen.

You're making a big commotion over nothing.

No, I'm not. You haven't noticed before now? Did they just get like this? How well do you know this boy? Something's off about him. He's twisted in his seat since he sat down. And what about you? Why are you so pasty-looking?

I told her that I hadn't noticed the blue until that morning, and that I knew Stanton well, though not too well. And although he'd had the jitters since I'd met him, I told her that she'd squirm and jitter too if she was under the kind of gaze she'd trapped him under. And as for myself, I said I couldn't account for my skin, although I swore I'd been eating square meals.

Stanton came back in directly and we left back for Richmond. I had him ride by Sade and Amanda's houses and toot the horn, according to my mother's instruction. In spite of his lips, she was anxious for her friends to know that I had a sport with an automobile. She told me to drive by only. She was very firm about this. She didn't want to fend off Sade and Amanda's lip curiosity all week. *Don't stop and go in. They can see he's good-looking enough from the road. Okay?*

Stanton and I made casual conversation all the way to

Virginia, but I couldn't find the right way to ask any questions. I did notice how much he jittered, though, which I hadn't really thought about until my mother pointed it out. But I tried not to think about any of it. He was so good-looking. I didn't want to rock the boat and turn 1939 into the year known as the year Betty tried and failed to have a young man.

He let me off at the rooming house and I went in and studied, thinking everything was pretty normal otherwise. And then I didn't see nor hear from him all week, which was very unusual. I started to worry about his welfare, although half of me wondered if he'd gotten home after our trip and decided to bail out. So I was half worried about him for his well-being and half worried for mine. Then a few more days passed and all my worry melted into sheer anger.

About the time I was ready to throw up my hands I got a telephone call downstairs from a hospital nurse with a message from Stanton. The message was to bring him a carton of cigarettes. I asked this lady what in the world he was doing in the hospital, and she told me very curtly, He's sick.

She cut me off in a rude manner, and there I was faced

with the task of delivering a carton of Luckies to the hospital for someone who I hadn't heard from in over a week. I wasn't overworried about his health at that point. If he could smoke, he surely wasn't near death or even under an oxygen tent.

I got myself in gear and made the purchase and off I went. Before I went to his ward, though, I stopped at the nurse's station and inquired about his illness. Naturally I feared stepping out into the unknown. What I was told was that Stanton had been brought in with acetanilid poisoning, apparently from going overboard with Neurol Compound, and he'd been in bad shape, though now he'd turned the corner. The nurse went on to say that he was just down the hall, in his usual room. His usual room! She went on to explain that Stanton was a patient on this particular dope ward about twice, sometimes three times a year. I'm sure she assumed I loved to indulge as well.

Yes, I was stunned. But then all those regulators and pep pills floated up, and I thought, Thank goodness I had the will not to get hooked. I was embarrassed at my stupidity, thinking he was doing me a favor. But what of this Neurol Compound? I had witnessed Stanton taking enough of these remedies, frankly, to kill a horse. I told him once that anybody whose head popped and rang to that extent should go see a doctor, but I was made to feel funny for caring enough to say anything, thus I backed off.

So on in I went to see him. He saw me coming and shouted to me like he'd spotted me in a crowd at the ballpark. He yelled, Hey, girlie! You sure look swell! Bring me those cigs!

He was sitting up and looked fairly healthy, though weak-eyed. And his lips looked fine as well, nice and pink. I slammed his cigarettes on the nightstand and said outright, I refuse to believe I've been going with a dope fiend.

He said, Then, girlie, you shouldn't believe it. He more or less snickered between his teeth. Chee, chee, chee.

I said, Listen, you need to get well and get your life in order. I told him I'd discovered he was a regular on the dope ward, which didn't embarrass him as it would anybody with scruples. And I said as well that I was humiliated over having swallowed all his lies, plain and fancy.

He had something sneering to say about how fast I trotted downtown with his cigarettes, to which I replied that if he was such a big man why didn't he pick up the phone and order me down there himself? Why'd he make a nurse call me?

Then I left, hearing him yell for me all the way to the steps, Hey, girlie! Come back, girlie! The fact of him calling me girlie hadn't bothered me until then, and walking to the rooming house I had to think of what my mother had told me. And I sat out on the stoop a great while trying to think if the young man had ever called me by name. I convinced myself he had, though to be honest, I'm not sure if he had or he hadn't. He seemed worlds away from the young man who had first bowled me over in front of my register at Kresge's. And then two thoughts twirled through my mind and kept me up a long while that evening. Could I have been that bad a judge of character, and what will I tell my mother?

The next morning I wrote home and told her the truth. I simply had to. Then I cried miserably and went to bed, wondering if I'd be better off simply married to Luther Miracle, chopping his cotton and nursing his children, cooking his suppers in spite of his obnoxious mother and his locks and locks of dirty hair.

My mother wrote back right away and told me to consider coming home, if for no other reason than my own safety.

Dear Betty,

Just a note. So many young people are going to the bad these days and if you don't consider yourself strong enough to keep out of trouble living the high life then you should come home in spite of the fact that you may think I'm just trying to get you back here and as well Polly Deal talks continuously and I need somebody here to help me listen to her.

Love,

Your mother Lottie

I wrote her back and said I wanted to stay in Richmond and make the best of things, and I apologized if this broke her heart. However, as soon as I got home from the post office I started packing like the house was on fire, and in twelve hours I was on my way out of Richmond, Virginia, where sin was and probably still is very, very handy.

Needless to say, my mother was glad to see me. Polly Deal was as well, although she told me right away that she'd moved into my bedroom and was comfortable to the point of contentment. She was very quiet, looking straight at me, waiting until I finally said, Well, you stay right there then and I'll move in the room with my mother.

She didn't thank me. She merely said, If I look in a weakened state, it's because some folks have upset my constitution and made my misery their daily intent. Then she excused herself to my bedroom, locked the door, and cranked the radio up.

I asked my mother what was wrong with Polly, and I was told she'd had a row with a town lady of some means who'd heard tales of Polly's touch with fine laundry and looked to hire her.

So this lady sent out her son with a bundle, which Polly did in good order and sent back and all was well. And then here's this lady showing up in my yard, getting Polly out around where I couldn't see from the window, involving Polly in a horrible dispute. She left, and Polly ran past me and locked herself up and wouldn't talk, not at first, though later she came in my room and crawled right in the bed with me and cried, saying that this woman had slapped her in the face for scorching her pet handkerchief. This was a bad, bad thing to see happening to her. I'd never seen her like this. She went to sleep right with me. Right with me! This was not the modest Polly Deal I knew. And then she woke up in the morning mad at the world, swearing off all but her own laundry in protest.

All she'll do is cook now, and not with a great deal of

*enthusiasm anymore, and then sit in the room with the
radio blaring, waiting to be engaged for a birthing, packing
and repacking her little medical satchel. And if she's not
doing this, she talks and talks and rambles and rambles.
Polly is simply not herself.*

So, added to the natural reason my mother was glad to
see me was this fact of Polly swearing off laundry. When
my mother said she'd been handed the task of doing her
own things plus the Woodliefs' things as we'd promised, I
said, Well, I know this has been wearing you out. But then
she took me to the laundry porch and showed me piles
and mounds and heaps of everything she just hadn't been
able to talk herself into doing. Thus I changed into a
shirtwaist and dug back in on Milk Farm Road.

But, not to leave Stanton in the air in Richmond—I
didn't intend to keep up with him once I left there. I didn't
love him as I had, especially after seeing his true colors
revealed to me on the dope ward. But he found a replace-
ment very quickly. Fast men always do.

A few days after I got home I got a letter from one of
my Kresge's girlfriends saying she'd seen Stanton on the
street that morning. He and his new girl were thrashing
out their personal business in front of a gallery row of

onlookers. They both looked ready for a shroud. She was a very frazzled young thing and had on a garish dress and white shoes in spite of October. That's what he was reduced to after me.

And then I wasn't home three months before she wrote me with the news that Stanton had dropped dead from being too high off aromatic spirits of ammonia. Of course I was still angry and embarrassed over Richmond, but I was also very sad. Sometimes Stanton had a way of treating me so kindly. Sometimes he pleased me better than I could please myself.

My mother saw me reading and wanted to see the letter, and after she read it she sat by me on the sofa. *If you and him had stayed together just think of how broken up you'd be right now! Whew!*

Then she took my hand and rubbed and patted it in her old way and told me that I'd returned home just in time, in the nick of time. *Honey, there's somebody due back next week from Dismal Swamp who might interest you. From all reports, he's been out there getting better looking every day, and smarter.*

16. *Of Betty's success in courtship*

"THE SOMEBODY BACK WAS HERMAN RANDOLPH, the son of the man who had rented our acreage and the mill after my father died. Herman and I had been in school together, but like so many other boys he had failed to catch my attention. However, he had traveled from home and been more or less molded by his experiences with the W.P.A., as would any young man given the task of dredging out the Great Dismal Swamp. But then in the fall of 1939 his father called Herman back to Milk Farm Road, thus putting an end to his twenty-five-dollar-a-week bonanza.

Herman and I always enjoyed remembering the morning he came home. I was helping my mother, his mother, named Mary Jo, and Amanda Bethune grade tobacco. This was the one farming task my mother would do, as it was clean and could be done sitting down while talking. We'd started out the morning arguing over insignificance, but by lunchtime we were onto whether or not America should become wrapped up in the foreign problem.

I mentioned something about Hitler, and Herman's mother said, We ought to've killed him in the last war. Amanda and my mother both agreed, saying we'd have to go over and straighten out Europe again. *We'll root him out this time.*

I was amazed to have to tell them that Hitler was not held over from the World War, that they apparently had Hitler mixed up with the Kaiser.

They shot back that they were not confused, that I was. Then my mother reminded me how much she and Polly Deal listened to the radio. They did! But as soon as the news came on they'd get in a huff and flip through looking for singing.

They all thrashed the Hitler problem around some more and then Herman appeared at the door, fresh from the W.P.A. He was wearing pincheck britches and a tweed cap, and when he took off his cap his hair was dirty, which cast my mind to Luther Miracle. Herman still looked better than Luther, though. He had a thoughtful face.

Mary Jo looked up at the door and laid her leaves down and spoke to Herman in anything but a motherly fashion. She said, Well, I see you got home. Then she told him his hat was ugly, and he folded it into his pocket.

Of course, he wanted to know why his mother wasn't more pleased to see him, and I explained the controversy. And of course, he told them I was right, which pleased me. Then I grabbed my sweater and excused myself, wondering if he'd follow me outside. He did.

He kept pace beside me and said, Listen, when are you planning to bring back my gramophone? His sister had written to tell him that he'd be returning home to no gramophone.

I said, That machine was given to me by your mother and father for my graduation. Had he graduated? I asked.

No, he said. He told me that while I was enjoying an illegal gramophone, he was out making a contribution.

I lacked the nerve to comment on the matter of his twenty-five-dollar-a-week take-home. But I did realize at this point that Herman viewed himself as somewhat more than he was, having the gift of gab and so forth, and that I'd have to check this in his nature. Having suffered under this reputation for quite some time myself, I knew Herman's mind well, though he believed I was more or less duped.

I said to him, Listen, if you want that machine you'll have to come get it.

He came to my house that evening meaning to cart it away, but he said he'd let me keep it if I'd go with him to the picture. I thought this was very cute, if transparent. But I let him take me. And then I kept letting him. Trudy had my mother watch her children some nights and we all three went out together. She remarked once that Herman wasn't as bright as I was, and I thought, oh gosh, to do better I'd have to fly off again and I just don't have it in me.

Nobody, the least of which my mother, was surprised by the amount of time Herman and I began to spend with each other. Never having taken real company with anyone except Stanton, I swung headlong into this indeed.

Herman and I had a daily routine. He would work with his father until dark, eat one supper at home and then come over here and pretend he hadn't eaten so he could eat another supper with me. My mother brought this to my attention. I'd assumed he was passing up his mother's table for me. *Honey, every night when he gets here he smells like food. Haven't you noticed? I know his mother served cabbage five nights running. She fries a great deal of fish as well.*

We did everything a typical couple does falling in love. We sat around, went to the picture, listened to the gramophone, which I had drawn a hard line over. I used to sing like a sheer bird for Herman. He had such a kind way of showing how impressed he was by me. Even after I'd stripped off his layers of gab, I could tell he was moved. I'd sing and clap:

> Where did you get that pretty dress,
> All so bright and gay?
> I got it from my loving man on the W. P. and A.
> On W. P. and A., on W. P. and A.,
> I got it from my loving man on W. P. and A.

And then it would go on and on and he'd sing:

When I die just dig a hole
Way down beneath the clay.
And tell them all I killed myself
On W. P. and A.

Polly Deal at one point brought something up, noticing as she had that I was in love. She asked me what I was doing to guard myself.

I said, Nothing! which she interpreted as risking all and playing with danger. But I actually meant that I had no call for anything, so thus I used nothing. As with Stanton, I'd kept my two feet in my two shoes flat on the ground, although with Herman I'd not been given the chance to test my will. He'd been a gentleman. But I knew this could change at any moment.

Polly went to the spice cabinet and came back with a jar of alum, saying I could use it in combination with tansy tea or simply by itself, though it'd work best teamed with the tea. But remember, she told me, stay away from black haw roots, which makes the little ones hold on even tighter.

I of course distrusted the idea of guarding myself with a stinging pickling spice, and the only other information I had on the matter dealt with the dasher. When I asked my mother about all this, she set her face and told me, *You'd better not have a baby.* She wouldn't tell me the best way to go about not having one, but I got the message that I'd better use the true common sense way to avoid such luck. Thus, when Herman finally did whisper his wants in my ear, I whispered back, Honey, in that case there'll have to be a ring on my finger.

17. *The decision is made*

"WHEN HITLER REALLY STARTED TRAMPLING all over Europe, I sat Polly Deal and my mother down one night and made them listen to a news story about Hitler's history, and then I said, See? Hear what he said?

My mother said, Oh, Mary Jo really had him confused. Then they flipped around like they always had for the music.

And then shortly after this we were bombed, all very suddenly. Naturally, this was all Herman cared to talk about. He came to pick me up for a picture and then tried to fool me into going to the Dinette instead and discussing what he called his new future. I refused the Dinette and campaigned hard for the picture. I didn't want to talk about him getting killed, which shows how little faith I had he'd come back home a hero. He simply wasn't cut of this cloth. But this isn't to say I didn't root for my country. I simply felt worried for Herman and ill-convenienced by the whole affair. It wasn't like I'd enjoyed a string of young men. The entire ordeal made me feel more or less hopeless in this regard.

I finally had my way and off we went to the picture. We watched *Andy Hardy's Private Secretary*, with Herman very disinterested throughout. For some reason he disliked Mickey Rooney and he took all his pictures very personally. He loved Charlie Chan, though, better than anything in the world. I didn't. I remember I used to sit in those Charlie Chan pictures and get so bored I'd clean my purse out in the dark. It got to the point that if my purse became unbearably messy, I'd say, Well, Mr. Chan must be coming out with another picture.

Herman didn't have to enlist. He was farming, which excused as many young men as asked to be let out of the war. Even my father had used pacifism as an excuse and begged out of World War I. But Herman set his course and neglected to tell me. I was over by Amanda's one afternoon, and she popped out with, I guess Herman finally settled his mind on the Navy.

Of course, I had to say I didn't know.

I dashed home and started writing Herman a letter. I was so mad I couldn't talk fast enough explaining my state of mind to my mother. She stood over my shoulder at the table and tried to tell me what to say to Herman, interfering at every pause and comma. I told her that if she could do it better then I'd give her the pencil and she could do it herself.

Anybody else's mother would have merely sighed and walked off, but mine took the pencil from me and snatched a fresh sheet of paper out of my ledger and wrote this letter. I just watched. She said:

Dear Herman,

Just a note. I have heard this morning that you have joined the navy Swell Is this true? I'm telling you if you signed up to go to the navy you are going to hate it. You may not now sonny boy but you will later on I wouldn't think you would join the navy. My mother is very surprised and she thought I'd been going with somebody with better sense than to join the navy to be shot at in the water. Its not so smart to me either since everybody in the world knows you cant swim three feet. Although you may be mad about something you did not have to join the navy to get pleased. This is just what I have heard today so if you have not joined please do not pay attention to it.

Love
Betty

Her letter was as good as anything I could've written, and I'd forgotten he couldn't swim. She urged me to keep telling her how good and to the point her letter was. I finally pulled away from her and ran and stuck it in the Randolphs' door and waited at home until Herman dropped his reply on our steps and dashed. My mother and I fairly raced each other out there and stood and read what he said. He wrote this on the bottom of our letter. He said:

Dear Betty,
It is not my falt if I care about America. Yes I am in the navy now or will be next month and I may stay in

the milaterry but you are still swell but you make me mad.

Love,
Herman Randolph

We stayed out there picking apart his note, for instance his signing his last name. And we both had to wonder if the Navy would teach him how to spell military. Then I put the letter in my pocket and walked back to our house, and I stopped to think and I asked my mother what she thought. She said I should marry him before he left for Japan and then keep living with her and Polly Deal, and that way we all would be pleased.

18. *An account of the celebrations, with a further account of what happened afterwards*

"MY WEDDING DRESS, THOUGH PRETTY, WASN'T what one usually has in mind. It was merely one I had and loved, and lacking time to contact Butterick's, remade thoroughly in a few evenings. I scooped the bodice to the point that Mary Jo Randolph swallowed hard during my preview and suggested a nice piece of lace inlay, which I declined. I doubted I'd ever again have the opportunity to dress up to this extent, knowing as I did the dressing habits of those whose lot was cast for Milk Farm Road. My mother told Mary Jo in short that she'd been invited over for a little coffee cake wedding preview to more or less compliment, not criticize, my efforts. I was appalled by Herman's mother, although when I next called attention to the refashioned leg-o-mutton sleeves, all I got were raves.

I'd wanted to decline a bridal shower, but my protests were overridden by all. The engagement was on the short side, this side of three weeks, barely enough time to throw a wedding together, not to mention a party. But a modest party we had on a Sunday afternoon, with Herman's mother serving as hostess in spite of my own mother's wishes. She managed however to squeeze Polly Deal into the affair under the pretense of service, sending the main Randolph help into town for the day. This was the only way we knew that Polly could come. However, the Randolph home was much nicer than ours, more gadgets and confusing electrical doodads and what-have-you, including a servants' button in the dining room that Polly accidently stepped on a thousand times and trotted to the door expecting more guests, who sometimes were there but usually were not. Neither my mother nor I had the heart to tell Polly the definition of a servants' button and whispered to the others to keep mum as well.

The gifts were overwhelming. Celia came bearing potholders of her own design. Amanda brought me a set of three blue-rimmed ceramic bowls, at which time Herman's mother suggested I use these bowls to make Herman something nice to take on the boat with him. I was supposed to promise sweetly to do this, but the cat got my tongue. My mother spoke for me. She told Herman's mother that cooking for enlisted men was not my pleasure, and then on we were to the next gift.

Odessa had brought a beautifully woven wooden basket with scented soaps and embroidered hand towels, which everyone envied. But everyone also knew that before Odessa left she would whisper in my ear how she'd love to have the basket back, if I didn't mind. Her basket made its way around the Milk Farm Road community thousands of times.

Sade Duplin made me, of all things, an attic window quilt, which I broke down over, only to do likewise again when Trudy's children brought their gifts, a dirt dauber's nest, fresh guinea eggs, and a compact mirror, which my mother recognized as one she thought she'd long since dropped from a pocket. The children went as far as saying they'd forgotten they'd borrowed it, but would go no further, even in the spirit of the day. Nonetheless, my mother let them stay, in light of the other two thoughtful, well-meant gifts. Trudy wasn't the kind of person who gives gifts, so that was that for the Woodliefs. Several girls from my school teamed up on a dinner slip for the Sir Walter Raleigh Hotel, which they thought just the place for our last meal before Herman shipped out.

With the exception of the Sir Walter meal and the Woodlief presents, everything else I received at the bridal was intended for one setting up housekeeping, which I wasn't planning to do now and had no real idea when I would. The overall plan was for Herman to go and come back and move in with my mother and me, and just basically for everything to more or less remain the same until I had a baby. Then we'd ask him to tack on more room, as had seemed to work in Kentucky.

So, unlike other young people organizing their own nests, I couldn't take all my gifts in a box in the truck to my new home. I put the potholders directly under my mother's sink, the soap on the edge of the tub, and the hand towels in the closet. They were too pretty to use that soon. The dirt dauber nest I put on my dresser, the fresh guinea eggs I put in the icebox, and the attic window quilt went across the foot of my bed. Everybody who gave me anything knew my situation, and thus wouldn't be offended to find their gifts used or displayed about in my mother's home. And these women frankly didn't know how to give any other gifts. Celia always gave potholders, for example, so this is what I received. The same with Amanda's bowls. And my mother and I, for another example, always gave little scented oil lamps with etched globes. The bride could've been blind, but this is what my mother gave invariably.

The same women were back for the wedding, which took place in the living room, and while decorated to the hilt and scented sweetly with crushed winter savory from Polly's herb garden, it remained merely a room in a house. Polly was dressed as I'd never seen her. She appeared right before the ceremony began in a starched white dress with a brightly colored turban of kitchen towels and silk sashes twirled high on her head, looking very pointed towards a festival. The ceremony was in fact delayed a few minutes while Polly enjoyed everyone's comments.

Many other young women would've balked at the more or less ordinary arrangements in lieu of a large church affair, but I welcomed any pretty spot at all. And a church of any size was denied me as I'd never made a church home, having a mixed religious nature of Quaker and Catholic, appreciating both though trained in neither. So I was content to say my vows in front of our sunniest window, with tintypes of Sheamus and Bart and Bridget, her teeth and ten children looking down on me.

My mother more or less ran the range of all her emotions that day. Each time she moaned I reminded her that I was merely marrying and not running off. With this, she seemed to rein in a bit and show her cheer. But then she'd lapse. *This too will change! You watch! You'll come telling me that you and he need privacy in spite of the fact that the locks in this house work perfectly.* Then I'd call her attention to the nice food and cake and so forth and she'd take a deep breath and plow forward into the affair.

Right after the wedding supper, Herman and I went to White Lake for our honeymoon. He campaigned for this spot because it was pretty and near, not to mention full of fond memories from his Future Farmers of America camps. Since his father was paying for it, I felt like I ought to be able to go anywhere, with Warm Springs the particular place I had in mind. But train travel was tight and Herman in a hurry to get away, so off we went to White Lake with me trying to keep my chin up. He, as was only natural, felt like he had to make all sorts of promises for something better later, but I feared deeply settling for White Lake, seeing him off, him getting killed, and me there on Milk Farm Road with my mother and Polly Deal always sitting, sitting, sitting.

I'll have to say now, though, that the glass bottom boat ride was memorable. Taken at night in a romantic hue, it's the sort of thing that can make a woman forgive a young man for not taking her to Warm Springs. The boat was packed with war-ready couples like Herman and me, making do with looking down between our feet in the moonlight and stars, listening to the man on the talking horn describe the habits of catfish in the evening.

The only blue side to the affair was my constant struggle with the weak stays in the strapless my mother had made for me. I'd insisted on a strapless, although the temperature said long or at least quarter-length sleeves. The little jacket she'd forced on me held back no wind, so I spent a great deal of my honeymoon evening holding myself up shivering, and fighting off my new husband's kind offers of his tweed for fear of the blatant contrast in fabrics. I was told this was impractical by those on the boat, but a tweed is a tweed and a knit is a knit. I've since then tended to associate glass bottom boats with weak stays and the cold March wind and have certainly never since subjected myself to all three at once.

The rest of the honeymoon held many surprises, some I certainly expected and some I did not. But all in all everything was lovely, with the exception of Herman at times acting like White Lake was something he had to go through to get to Japan. Several times I had to pull him back in line and remind him to treasure the moment or check his desires to rant about the menace. Many other young women at White Lake Hotel that spring complained of this same ordeal. And if I had to be honest, the final imperfection in the entire honeymoon week was the startling news that I'd married a man who liked to snore in my face. But I went ahead and let him, knowing all he'd face in the coming year, and knowing as well that this was certainly something we could nip as soon as he got back home.

Soon after we returned to Milk Farm Road everybody ganged up at the train station to see Herman off. And not only Herman, but Amanda's oldest son and several of the boys I'd declined in school. I had my feelings hurt somewhat that morning, trying to wish these boys well and wishing they'd have more to do with me. This simply mounded on the depression of it all. And Luther Miracle came with his mother and two young children and his friendly, wide-eyed wife from another county. My mother noticed that Luther had washed his hair and had more than likely been uplifted and saved by a conscientious woman.

19. *An ordeal after all, or all is well*

"AND THEN THERE CAME ANOTHER TURN IN THE road! As shaky as I was on all other matters pertaining to childbirth, I was firm in my belief that I did not intend to suffer. Polly Deal had come home from deliveries and described the torment and several times the death and I saw no reason to go this route when Park View Hospital was a mere eight miles from my home.

Of course, Polly Deal was miffed. She'd expected to be automatically engaged for the delivery when I first broke the news. But I said, Listen, Polly, unless you can knock me out completely and wake me up with a baby, I'm going to Park View. Several women I knew had gone there and had themselves put under Twilight Sleep and never felt a thing. They reported waking up insane and coming in and out of their minds for three days afterwards, but the point remains that they didn't hurt.

But Polly more or less persecuted me for weeks, mumbling barely loud enough for me to hear her, counting off how many babies she'd safely delivered, saying the delivery room and nursery ward were things white men had thought up as a new way to trick money out of foolish women. Then she would remark how good a value and convenience she was, especially now during war-time with gasoline so tight.

My mother urged me to flip a coin, which I saw as a very haphazard way of deciding my fate. *Flip a coin! End the matter! Polly will addle us otherwise. This way she'll at least feel like she was given a chance.* But I couldn't flip. Herman wrote voting for the hospital, hinting that this was certainly the way to go as my mother would be paying for it. His mother thought it was a great extravagance, though true to form for my mother and me. So I stood my ground against Polly's services, and I bore with her mumbling about her official license, her safety record, and all the various day-after services that she'd throw in free of charge.

I insisted that the baby shower not be as all-out as the bridal. I really saw no point in all the women hoarding sugar for one short afternoon's pleasure. Thus we had something small after a card game during my seventh month, at which I received all grades of advice, as well as many little crocheted items.

I was having a lovely time until the chit-chat turned to Herman. He was on board the *Hornet* at this time, which if I believed all his letters was either on smoldering fire or about to explode a great deal of the time. His tales seemed so outlandish that sometimes I'd write back and remind him that I didn't need this added tension and to check his gift for gab if he would.

And then Trudy had me convinced that by raising my arms above my head I would strangle the baby and thus for a time I refused to get plates out of the cabinet, fill the bird feeder, and roll my own hair. Needless to say, if this sort of silly worry concerned me, one can imagine that the vision of my new husband's boat on fire in the ocean caused me many nights of restless alarm.

I worried about this and everything else while I was carrying. Sometimes my mother would drag me out of the house and instruct me to walk off my tension, and thus I'd trail miserably along behind her up and down Milk Farm

Road. Sometimes for a change of scenery she would keep the Woodlief children while I sat with Trudy at the pictures and tried not to think. My mother would scrub the children to the point of chapped redness while we were gone, and as well she would train them to speak out of character. They'd say, We had a wonderful bath. The water was nice and tepid. Was the picture to your liking?

After all my outings, Polly encouraged me to drink black haw root tea, boiled to quarter cups and by far strong enough to trot mice on. She convinced me that black haw root made babies hang on tighter. She said, Once you get to your hospital, if the baby has a time letting go, be sure and tell the doctor about the black haw so he can switch you over to tansy and loosen you. I felt compelled to promise to do this.

Polly Deal probably got her wish because she willed it so, on the strength of her fiery nature. She probably woke up two days after Thanksgiving of 1942 and said, I intend for Betty Davies Randolph to cause a flood in the kitchen and fall into fast labor and let me find her too far gone to haul to the hospital after all.

I was in the midst of a nice plate of leftover Thanksgiv-

ing when my situation began. I had no way of knowing if
the situation were real or merely cause for embarrassment,
as there was nobody in the house to ask. My mother was
out of the house for the afternoon looking after the smaller
Woodliefs for Trudy to take the older ones shoe shopping,
and Polly had disappeared off right behind her.

I left my food half done and organized myself enough
to call the doctor, whose nurse said to sit and wait for him
to return the call, which I did. I sat and sat and sat, growing uncomfortable and scared to the point that I chewed
off my beautiful nails, polish and all, and cried myself
breathless. I wondered if I could make my way all the
distance down to Trudy's house, and then I hemmed and
hawed, debating with myself until this was out of the question. In short, I was stuck. And who could I call? Trudy
certainly had no telephone, and the store telephone had
been tied up with worried women since Pearl Harbor.
And Sade and Amanda and Herman's mother? No answer. Just ring, ring, ring! I was frankly desperate to the
point that I considered standing out in the yard and
flagging strange cars off of Milk Farm Road. Ambulances,
for us, were unknown.

I tried the doctor again. Ten minutes apart by then I

was and showing no signs of slacking off. And once again, he was not in, though I was told he'd call me the first chance he got.

I asked the nurse, Did I mention to tell you I've broken?

She said, Yes, honey, just be patient. She made over the situation more or less like I'd have to learn to wait my turn.

I hung up and cried, thinking, What if this baby doesn't want to wait its turn? Suppose I have a pushy little baby? This was certainly a running trait in my family.

Polly came humming in the door when I was about five minutes apart and not feeling very well at all, nauseous and confused and wondering which would finally kill me, the pain or the bleeding. My dream had been to lie down in a beautifully clean hospital room and smile up at my good-looking doctor there ready to put me under the gas. I dreamed I'd count backwards and trail off and then open my eyes later to my baby all ready for me. My dream was not Polly coming in and taking her muddy fishing boots off in the kitchen, yelling through the closed door at me, Betty! What's all that wailing? You'll be wailing soon enough!

I yelled back, Polly! Hush! Come help me! It's now!

I heard her scramble, scramble around changing her shoes. Then she yelled that she was washing the fish off of her. I thought, Good God!

Of course, the water seemed to run an hour. But when the sound stopped, Polly Deal appeared at the parlor door and I told her how glad I was she was with me and how scared I'd been and so forth. She said, Why aren't you in the bed? Why aren't you in something clean to wear? Why are you propped up by the telephone?

I told her about waiting on the doctor, hating to, knowing she'd pounce on me.

She said, Suppose you called him during his dinner hour? Do you think he'd budge up from a china plate to go to work? Suppose he's got other babies going all over town at the same time? I told you the story way back. And now I suppose you want to yank me up at the last minute to deliver yours on out. Well!

Then she told me I should've gotten out some clean sheets and water and so forth and made plans to deliver the baby myself if called to, and she said I wouldn't be the first nor the last young mother to rely on her own authority.

I wondered if Polly Deal would let me die on the parlor daybed sheerly because I'd not reserved her instead of the hospital, and I thought and thought and finally said, Listen, Polly, I'll pay you what I was planning to pay Park View. Okay?

She didn't say anything at all to me. She turned down the hall and reappeared in a moment with her hair tied in a white scarf, with a burden of white sheets. She sat down by me and felt of me all around and counted my times. Then she told me that by the pink of the evening we'd have a new baby.

Even though I knew I'd be more comfortable in the bedroom I told her I preferred to go through the rest of the ordeal right there on the daybed. It seemed like a great deal more trouble than it was worth to get up and go down the long hall. So thus I settled in for the afternoon with all the O'Cadhains witnessing such a large event once more from their place on the wall.

Where's your mama? Polly asked me, rolling me over, making the bed up under me.

She's still at Trudy's tending to the children, I said. I told her I wished she would trot down the hill and bring her home.

Polly bent close to my face and whispered a very strong secret. She said, Let's leave her there. Let's let her stay as long as she will. Let's born the baby just us. It's easier without a mother at a borning. Young girls will wonder and look to their mothers to see if they're doing something wrong. It's no right and wrong, though. But I've seen young girls look for their mama to tell them when they're supposed to hurt and stop hurting. And I think that you as much as anybody needs to do this one thing this time without Miss Lottie.

I knew I needed to do what she said. And so I gave in and I rolled in and out of Polly's arms as she finished making the daybed with a great cushion of sheets under me with an extra fold in the small of my back, and each time I rolled I gave in more to her care.

Polly Deal caught the baby a few minutes before six o'clock. I saw all and felt all, and of course the baby wasn't handed to me washed and wrapped all tucked around. But naturally, she was pretty as is, and I held and loved her right away. Then Polly wrapped her around in the sheet of white muslin she had warmed in the oven. Wrapping the baby around, she asked me about the name, asking me in such a fashion that advised me to name the baby Polly Something or Something Polly. I said the baby's name was Marjorie Polly, two names that go together not at all. I'd intended to name the baby Marjorie Eileen, but Eileen was sacrificed.

Polly seemed pleased. Then she fussed around in her satchel a minute and fished out the eyedrops and told me to hold the baby while she put in the drops. The baby was fussing a great deal but Polly got the drops in, singing her song:

> We put drops in the baby's eyes
> Whether the mother laughs or cries,
> The State for us the drops buys,
> As we go marching on.

Then she gave me the baby back and went fishing in her satchel again, bringing out this time a little blue perfume-looking bottle, which she put at my mouth and said to blow, blow, blow. I blew, not knowing why. I asked when I'd blown enough to suit her and was told that if I didn't blow in the blue bottle that whatever afterbirth was left inside would mortify and I would never stop hurting.

She said, Some women always hurt and now you know why.

Then she laid the baby across my stomach and looked at her good all over. Polly said she needed to do something about the baby's head, which happened to go up in back into sort of a windblister point. She told me she would get to the head in time.

This head, she told me, has to wait on the book work.

She got out a little pad of blank slips and wrote and nodded, singing:

> We report births and deaths and all
> When anything is wrong, we the doctor call,
> We hope we never from grace may fall,
> As we go marching on.

After she finished writing she read back to me, Caught one white baby girl, November 25, 1942, mother and baby both living. Baby named Marjorie Polly Randolph.

She made me drink horehound tea even though I told her I disliked it. And she also made me dip my finger in the cup for the baby to suck. We all rested for a bit and allowed the baby to settle down, and when Polly believed the time had come she said she intended now to fix the baby's head.

I asked her how. As a new mother, this concerned me somewhat.

Polly told me, There's not much to fixing a baby's head.

And then I watched her work, moving her hands all

around on the baby's head, shaping it like a ball of dough, and the little head got rounder and rounder, as round as you please. Then Polly took her hands away and stepped back and declared, "Now it looks like a head!"

She said if I was careful not to let the baby lay too much on one side of her head that she would always be smart and pretty. And she also made me promise to keep the baby out of the wind. The ears, she told me, are the most important parts of a baby. I said I'd do everything just so.

She dressed Marjorie Polly in the things my mother had ironed herself and set aside on top of the cedar chest. Two white petticoats and a white dress of piqué, all a yard long from the neck, two knit shoes and a white crocheted hat. And then Polly brought my baby and put her by me in the crook of my arm and whispered that she would walk down the hill and tell my mother all was done.

I told her the baby and I would be well and fine alone, and out Polly went for my mother. I felt of the baby's warm head and watched her eyes and soon we were asleep."

December 15, 1989

*My grandmother let Polly Deal trade her place babysitting,
and quickly she ran up the hill to see me just an hour old.
From all reports, she loathed the name Marjorie Polly and
campaigned for something with more character. But the story
of Polly Deal rescuing my birth was so famous by midnight
that my singular name was all but carved in stone.*

*I stayed in the house with my mother and grandmother
and Polly Deal, and from further reports thrived on all the
attention. All of us waited together for my father to come
home, and when he finally did I was two.*

*I wish I could say that my first memory is of my father
coming through the door, but I can't. The first true memory
is sound. All sorts of sounds above my cradle, maybe moving
with shadows of hands and shoulders, maybe my mother's
face shape. But certainly there were the sounds, faint and
loud and then shrill. Then, Hush! She's sleeping. Let her
sleep.*

*But I wasn't sleeping, not for the sounds of the women
talking.*

M. P. R.

Also available from Vintage Contemporaries

• •

Picturing Will
by Ann Beattie

An absorbing novel of a curious five-year-old and the adults who surround him.

"Beattie's best novel since *Chilly Scenes of Winter*... its depth and movement are a revelation." —*The New York Times Book Review*

0-679-73194-6

Latecomers
by Anita Brookner

A glowing novel about the ambiguous pleasures of friendship and domesticity, tracing the friendship between two men over a period of forty years.

"An extraordinarily eloquent novel, full of pleasures as well as lessons."
—*The New York Times Book Review*

0-679-72668-3

Where I'm Calling From
by Raymond Carver

The summation of a triumphant career from "one of the great short-story writers of our time—of any time" (*Philadelphia Inquirer*).

0-679-72231-9

The House on Mango Street
by Sandra Cisneros

Told in a series of vignettes stunning for their eloquence—the story of a young girl growing up in the Hispanic quarter of Chicago.

"Cisneros is one of the most brilliant of today's young writers. Her work is sensitive, alert, nuanceful... rich with music and picture." —Gwendolyn Brooks

0-679-73477-5

Wildlife
by Richard Ford

Set in Great Falls, Montana, a powerful novel of a family tested to the breaking point.

"Ford brings the early Hemingway to mind. Not many writers can survive the comparison. Ford can. *Wildlife* has a look of permanence about it." —*Newsweek*

0-679-73447-3

Ellen Foster
by Kaye Gibbons

The story of a young girl who overcomes adversity with a combination of charm, humor, and ferocity.

"Ellen Foster is a southern Holden Caulfield, tougher perhaps, as funny...a breathtaking first novel." —Walker Percy

0-679-72886-X

The Chosen Place, the Timeless People
by Paule Marshall

A novel set on a devastated part of a Caribbean island, whose tense relationships—between natives and foreigners, blacks and whites, haves and have-nots—keenly dramatize the vicissitudes of power.

"Unforgettable...monumental." —*Washington Post Book World*

0-394-72633-2

Keep the Change
by Thomas McGuane

The story of Joe Starling: rancher, painter, and lover, and his struggle to right himself.

"I don't know of another writer who can walk McGuane's literary high wire. He can describe the sky, a bird, a rock, the dawn, with such grace that you want to go see for yourself; then he can zip to a scene so funny that you laugh out loud."
—*The New York Times Book Review*

0-679-73033-8

Bright Lights, Big City
by Jay McInerney

Living in Manhattan as if he owned it, a young man tries to outstrip the approach of dawn with nothing but his wit, good will and controlled substances.

"A dazzling debut, smart, heartfelt, and very, very funny." —Tobias Wolff

0-394-72641-3

Friend of My Youth
by Alice Munro

Ten miraculously accomplished stories that not only astonish and delight but also convey the unspoken mysteries at the heart of human experience.

"She is our Chekhov, and is going to outlast most of her contemporaries."
—Cynthia Ozick

0-679-72957-7

Mama Day
by Gloria Naylor

This magical tale of a Georgia sea island centers around a powerful and loving matriarch who can call up lightning storms and see secrets in her dreams.

"This is a wonderful novel, full of spirit and sass and wisdom." —*Washington Post*

0-679-72181-9

Mile Zero
by Thomas Sanchez

A dazzling novel of American disillusionment and reawakening, set in Key West—the island that defines the end of the American road.

"A magnificent tapestry. Sanchez forges a new world vision…rich in the cultural and literary intertextuality of Steinbeck and Cervantes, Joyce and Shakespeare."
—*Los Angeles Times*

0-679-73260-8

Anywhere But Here
by Mona Simpson

An extraordinary novel that is at once a portrait of a mother and daughter and a brilliant exploration of the perennial urge to keep moving.

"Mona Simpson takes on—and reinvents—many of America's essential myths… stunning."   —*The New York Times*

0-679-73738-3

The Joy Luck Club
by Amy Tan

"Vivid…wondrous…what it is to be American, and a woman, mother, daughter, lover, wife, sister and friend—these are the troubling, loving alliances and affiliations that Tan molds into this remarkable novel." —*San Francisco Chronicle*

"A jewel of a book." —*The New York Times Book Review*

0-679-72768-X

Philadelphia Fire
by John Edgar Wideman

"Reminiscent of Ralph Ellison's *Invisible Man*" *(Time)*, this powerful novel is based on the 1985 bombing by police of a West Philadelphia row house owned by the Afrocentric cult Move.

"A book brimming over with brutal, emotional honesty and moments of beautiful prose lyricism." —Charles Johnson, *Washington Post Book World*

0-679-73650-6

• •

V I N T A G E
CONTEMPORARIES

VINTAGE
CONTEMPORARIES

V I N T A G E
CONTEMPORARIES

V I N T A G E
CONTEMPORARIES